Thumbnails

Gregory Norminton

Vagabond Voices
Glasgow

© Gregory Norminton 2013

First published in April 2013 by
Vagabond Voices Publishing Ltd.,
Glasgow,
Scotland

ISBN 978-1-908251-15-2

The author's right to be identified as author of this book under the Copyright, Designs and Patents Act 1988 has been asserted.

Printed and bound in Poland

Cover design by Mark Mechan

Typeset by Park Productions

The publisher acknowledges subsidy towards this publication from Creative Scotland

For further information on Vagabond Voices, see the website, www.vagabondvoices.co.uk

To Claire and Sebastiaan

Contents

Bad folks

Late flowers	11
Waxwings	13
Houghton triads	15
The return from exile of P. Ovidius Naso	18
Horse burial	21
Unforgetting	23
Goody goody	25
The carpenter's tale	27

The panic room in Eden

Gifts	31
The monumental achievement of José Rodrigues do Cabo	33
Pileup	35
The acid reef	37
From a dictionary of slang, circa 2050	40
The panic room in Eden	42
Stills from the Anthropocene Era	44
Visitors Book	48

All my little ones

Tête de veau	53
Singer	55
The kingdom upstairs	57
Intervention	59
The overnighters	61
Dormeus	63
Wild things	65
Bog man	68

Orpheus's lot

Orpheus's lot	73
Gorgon	75

Narcissus & the pool of mirrors	77
Preliminary report on the economics of unicorns	79
Cut is the branch	82
Glass slippers are a health hazard	85
The siren of May	87
Pearly Gates tick box survey	90

What gets lost

Bunking off	97
Cryptozoology	99
Sepiatone	101
One finger exercise	104
The runner	106
Time & the janitor	108
The Dirty Realist Choose Your Own Adventure Book	110
What gets lost	112

Bookends

Bibliophagy	117
Essential words of the Empress Shōtoku	119
A pillow book	121
The bard's last words	123
The translation of Archie Gloag	125
Flow	128
At prayer in the madhouse with Kit Smart	131
Endnotes	134

Bad folks

Late flowers

You should watch that one; she has ears like a hawk.

Arthur had come in to see me. She was in her armchair by the television. A man was on, showing things to do with parsley. Arthur parked his frame. His trusty steed, he calls it. Never mind her, I said. She's daft, there's nothing going on upstairs. Arthur's a gentleman. I noticed it the day we met. He likes to be proper. But I was sure we were safe and so we carried on.

Of course things would have been easier if we had rooms to ourselves. We do our best, screening our beds with photographs and rows of familiar trinkets, but it's not the same. Arthur had it worse than me. He shared with the Major. Poor circulation, bound to the settee. Made elephant noises in his sleep. I couldn't abide those unequal eyes, one shrivelled and one huge, like Ralph Richardson.

For a few weeks we were happy in mine. Always with Flora plumped in front of the box. Arthur got used to it and we came to forget all about her. When the Major died it took them a fortnight to replace him and then it was Mr Gads, who was quick on his feet. Arthur bribed him with whisky to make himself scarce.

So we left Flora to her cookery shows. And suddenly the game was up.

We were allowed special friendships. They were encouraged. But there have to be boundaries. Arthur's kids and mine heard about us from the Gorgon and had to interfere. They didn't want us tampering with our wills at this late stage.

What a fuss they made! I half expected the gentlemen from the press to appear with their flashbulbs. Barbara took me out to the garden. The camellias were in bloom. I said to her, look, they're lovely. Never mind about them, she said. It's not decent at your age. Not decent? I said. Just you wait, you'll be glad of the attention. The things she said. You don't like to think of your child's mind sprawling in the gutter.

From that point on we were under guard. Mr Gads was discouraged from going walkabout after lunch. He used to so enjoy his tour of the flowerbeds.

Our intimacy came to an end. They had tired Arthur out. We only hold hands now.

I wondered who it was gave the game away. There weren't many suspects. I had words with Flora about it. She smiled and patted my hand. I could have sworn I detected a glint in her eye.

It just goes to show about appearances. Who would have thought the old girl still had it in her?

Waxwings

The boy rubbed his cheek where it still throbbed. From the pinewoods he could hear the farting engines of dirt bikes.

After a time he found himself at the rear of the supermarket. There was a tree beside the bins. The boy heard the twittering but thought nothing of it until he saw the man.

"Hallo," the man said. He held binoculars. The boy did not run away because he wondered what the man was doing and the man said to him, "You are a lucky boy.

"Do you see those birds? It's a treat, you know; they hardly ever come to England." The man said they were waxwings on account of the red feathers like drops of sealing wax on the wings. Great flocks this winter had come across the North Sea. They came here for the berries: cotoneaster and rosehip and sloe. The tree pulsed with the birds and their chatter.

The boy felt the man's fingers when he showed him how to adjust the binoculars. Sorting through branches, the boy saw the little sharp birds and their raised crests but not their waxy feathers. The lens misted over and he handed the binoculars back. The bird man was smiling at the tree with the chattering birds in it.

The bikers came roaring, shitting mud, from the woods. They circled the tree with the birds and the bird man and the boy. In the diesel stink they left behind the man said, "People don't know the things they're given."

The boy took the knowledge home as a secret. It was something only he owned.

The next day he found the bird man and they went in search of the waxwings. The man pointed out other birds. The boy didn't know that the flickering ones are pied wagtails or that starlings do impressions like comedians off the telly.

Children surrounded him later with their bikes. Who was that man, they asked, but the boy kept his secret.

Someone must have spoken to mum. "Has he tried to touch you," she asked, "down there?" The boy felt his face burn. He set her straight but kept his secret.

The next day after school it wasn't mum stroking his hair but his stepdad who spoke to him. The boy's face burned for a different reason.

"You don't know *anything*. I like him better than you." Mum came in at the screaming. "Better than mum," he added.

Gossip spread among the houses. The man was divorced, he had recently moved to the estate. Nobody knew his business.

His step-dad came to fetch him from school but the boy got away. The bird man wasn't home so the boy went birdwatching on his own. He wandered far from the estate, along the main road, until Craig found him and drove him home.

After the assault the bird man was relocated by the council. For his own safety, the paper said.

Mum ironed the newspaper with her hand. "Well," she said, "if they took him away, there must have been something in it."

Houghton triads

Three desirable qualities in a Houghton male: a genial manner, a trustworthy face, stock options.

Three accomplishments acquired over time by Houghton women: social grace, an implacable smile, strategic incuriosity.

Three games played by Houghton children: I-spy, It, For God's Sake Go Outside.

Three hiding places: Mummy's walk-in wardrobe, the utility room, euphemism.

Three physical qualities to be desired of Houghton nannies: plainness, adaptability, a blind eye.

Three places of commerce: the organic farm shop, Harrods, Dubai.

Three places of leisure: Glyndebourne, Guards Polo Club, wherever she wants to go *this* week.

Three charities worth supporting: Shooting and Conservation, the Royal Lifeboats, the boys' future school.

Three places of business: the boardroom, the country house hotel, the strip club.

Three golfing skills required of a Houghton male: a carrying drive, a nifty pitch, the readiness to fluff a putt when politic.

Three avenues of escape from the Houghton lifestyle: retiring on the mother of all deals, downsizing to the country, a heart-attack at fifty.

Three elements of a sales pitch: technical language, flattery, acronyms.

Three words never to be used in a professional negotiation: bribe, minister, casualties.

Three items to bring home from a business trip: toys for the children, perfume for the wife, a plausible narrative.

Three indispensable brand names: Louis Vuitton, Bulgari, Botox.

Three preconditions for seduction: sleeping kids, a fine meal, demarcated exclusion zones in the conversation.

Three reasons to lie awake in the early hours: indigestion, fear of death, yesterday's news story.

Three items in the Houghton arsenal for dealing with journalists: assurance, silence, an aggressive lawyer.

Three stock words with which to dismiss the allegations: bosh, froth, piffle.

Three distractions from bosh, froth, piffle: a week in Klosters, a month in the Cotswolds, a night with an escort.

Three places of refuge for a Houghton wife: the club, the spa, the masseur.

Three consolations to offer Houghton children: Mummy loves you, teddy loves you, the pony.

Three best friends at a time of crisis: the Attorney General, the sheik, political expediency.

Three professional fallback options: a consultancy in Zurich, a think-tank in Washington, those contacts in Lagos.

Three expressions that brighten one's day: a surreptitious glance from a fitness instructor, smiles of reassurance from the legal team, the open mouths of protestors seen from a speeding car.

Three government assurances: the Saudis are unhappy, explanations are accepted, there is no need to prolong investigations.

Three lessons learned from the Houghton year: no lessons were learned from the Houghton year.

The return from exile of P. Ovidius Naso

To P.O. Naso – Rome

I hope this letter finds you safely returned from the working end of the empire which you once derided, and that you are renewing acquaintance with the fruits of that season for which you pined in a province where, in winter, the whole of nature displays but a single face. You see, I have read you well. It is as a reader that I permit myself to address you. I am, moreover, not unrelated to the source of your misfortune and its seeming correction, being close, exceedingly so, to the bookish runt of Drusus, mighty Livia's hobbling grandson. He it is who instructed me to compose this letter, that you might better understand the intentions of his step-uncle in returning you to Rome.

Many times, in the years following Augustus's judgement, I pictured you by the Euxine, writing in hope of reprieve or at least permission to transfer to a province where the sea cannot be walked upon in winter. Unlike some in this city, I trusted your accounts of the harsh steppe and barbarians as versed in our tongue as fish or bullocks. Deprived of wife and companions, with nothing to cheer you save bartered chunks of frozen wine, you listened out for the pounding of enemy hooves. I, that have never been fit to wear shield and armour, could only imagine you shivering on the battlements, waiting with your fellow settlers to defend the town that you hated less than the prospect of its capture. After such hardships, you must have wept with joy to be welcomed by our new Caesar back to the home which you had thought lost for ever.

Alas, your homecoming cannot prove a joyful one. Though you regain your villa and your house near the Capitol, you will find a cold welcome in the places of your triumphs and few traces of that eager audience which once acclaimed you. For Tiberius is a man who makes his deeper wishes plain and, though on the surface your faults are forgiven, yet all of Rome knows to keep out of your way.

It shall not be a challenge for citizens enamoured of novelty to overlook a white-haired, palsied old man. Suffering, they say, has left you ripped away from yourself, scarcely recognisable; and even your verses have not been spared. My appeals to the public libraries of Rome to reinstate your *Art of Love* have fallen on deaf ears. The one thing that kept your name fresh in the public's mind was your fate; and now that it has been revoked, I have heard men say: "He should have stayed in Tomis. We would have remembered him then."

Yet these gossips are deceived if they think your circumstances have changed; for it is not geography alone that can serve to exile a man. The farmer whose hills and crops have burned in a summer conflagration has not left home, yet home is ashes underfoot. In like fashion, Tiberius has decreed that your return to Rome be desolate; for the city where you triumphed will ignore you; it will be yours and not yours, the contrast between your former renown and your present oblivion more terrible to contemplate than any Sarmatian horde.

Ought you to regret the past that has brought you to this present? It is my belief that you could not have obeyed your Muse without incurring the wrath of those in authority. When Caesar Augustus, wanting a new Golden Age, tried to legislate against adultery, which is to say human nature, you would not pander to the idea and bruited it about that his own grand-daughter had a Vesuvius between her legs that no amount of offerings could propitiate. That tactless talent of yours spared nothing. You mocked the gods and maddened the Emperor, who is become a god; for none can read you and doubt that power fades, greatness corrupts and every accomplishment dissolves in time. Poets who seek an easy life know how to polish with words the rough timbers of power. This you did not do, and though a decade had passed since the publication of your erotic verses, I could have foretold that they would be used against you. The exposer of vice can easily be made to seem vicious by those who, wearing the mask of virtue, fear the revelation of the face beneath.

It affords me no pleasure to imagine the effect on you of this letter. I send it in order that you be forewarned and keep away from those humiliations that await you in Rome. Attempt, if you can, to reconcile yourself to fate, as must those of us that are born ill-made. Write, as I do, for your own pleasure, tend to your garden where your work is wanted, and take comfort in the knowledge that you will not be buried by the shores of that distant sea. Though you live in obscurity, entertain the hope that your verses may outlast us all. I remain, dear Ovid, that most elusive of creatures:

<blockquote>An admirer</blockquote>

Horse burial

The men came for us in the dead of night. A wind was blowing in from the Sea of Azov and our tents must have looked like great beasts huddled together against the cold. By then we were living beside the burial pit, where we expected to spend the next day brushing dust from the bones of horses. Semyon was pissing into the grass when he saw the guns. He made no sound. Nothing could have saved us.

Sometimes I wonder what it was like for the men who arrested us. They were drunk: you could smell it on their breaths. A few storm lanterns burned between our tents, giving just enough light for them to see the exhumed drinking cups cut from human skulls. Perhaps they viewed us with fear as the avatars of ancient shamans stooped over the remains of a sacrifice. But they were too habituated to relent. Even before their leader spoke, I felt myself age a thousand years.

One of my staff died in the prison where they crammed us forty to a cell designed for twelve. Anton Maximovich – who had come top of his year at the institute, who could recite Pushkin and Goethe and Shakespeare – was crushed against the bars. Semyon made it through to the cattle-trucks and we looked out for each other, for prisoners could be as savage as the guards and the *urkas* slept with murder in their fists.

"I can't understand it," Semyon said when our train had stalled for a week in the taiga. "We were doing good work – the *institute's* work. What changed while we were away?"

I have long ceased asking myself why. The man who seeks an answer to that question – an answer that makes any sense – soon finds himself eating shit with the goners. Best to accept it as you must the weather. In the early days, however, I still believed in reasons. What we had unearthed confirmed Herodotus on the Scythians: they did, indeed, make human sacrifices, which they buried among concentric rings of slaughtered horses. Civilised Russia, this seemed to confirm, had emerged from the barbarism and class inertia of nomads. I did not tell Semyon that he had made the mistake which doomed us. For in that same excavation we found shards of Greek pottery and

Persian jewels: confounding evidence of a cultural sophistication that could not please the Party. Semyon had written to the institute about it; he had even sent an article to the newspapers.

In our second year among the goldmines of Kolyma, Semyon must have understood all this, or else he did not mean to insult the man who tore out his throat.

Every one of my colleagues is dead and I remain – the ruin of our fellowship. Nor will I last long, for every day the blood tide rises in my chest, displacing all hope of breath.

I think about the Crimea. I am a city boy from the forested north: when I first went to the Black Sea, the steppe disturbed me. I long for it now, as I meditate on that burial pit.

We had no doubt that it marked an atrocity. We could not read the bones, only conjecture what suffering they attested to. Lying here, toothless, I wonder what archaeologists will make of these posts, these shacks and mine shafts, when in the future they come to exhume us.

Unforgetting

Hold yourself WELLCOME to the Monument of our Citizen Martyr! Show yourself respectful in the memory of 5000 killed on account of their ethnic being. Fifteen years after see live size models and dead photographs. Remember unforgettingly the victims of H— and leave generous givings for their monumental upkeep.

It was a goddamn ruin when we got there. The roof all caved in from the heat of the fire and rocks and stones all thrown in through the windows...
   (The local militia popped a number of them. It was like half the town was there.)
     I mean, Jesus, their own fucking building...
(All those loved ones – their photographs chewed up by the flames. Don't they respect their own dead?)
      The problem is these people do not want freedom. They do not understand what freedom is...
       (You ever seen so much melted wax?)
     These people hate freedom.
       (It's not like they needed a fire to keep warm.)

– I would not say: the crowd was all local people. Local people were *in* the crowd. That does not mean local people *were* the crowd. The crowd was infiltrated by foreign elements. Foreign elements manipulated the local people... That is the problem with foreign elements. Just when you know they are there, they are gone.

"It is with great sadness that I learned about yesterday's assault on the monument to the victims of H—. We all know... we can all see how sick this was. I feel this sick personally, because I was there. I was rewarded the honour of opening the monument three years ago. Since then people from around the world visiting H— have paid their respects to the victims of a brutal regime. We mustn't forget that one of the reasons we went in was to make sure this kind of thing… I'm referring to the massacre at H—… that this kind of thing never happens again. The former dictatorship was brutal. It didn't care about the people it murdered and that's something yesterday's extremists want to forget. Well I personally want to see the memorial rebuilt. It is vital for the people of H— that it be rebuilt because if we don't listen to the voice of the past how can we hope to build a good future?"

It is not so bad.

It looks worse than it is. The bullet passed through my leg. I will walk out of this hospital.

Listen.

Listen to me. For years they have promised us help. But the help has not come. There are no roads, no streets here, only mud.

They only took people to see the monument to the dead and never to see the living.

You see that man? That man in the chair by the window?
He has lost his son. It was his son who was killed.

He threw a stone.

Violence is bad. I do not approve of violence. Maybe we should not have attacked the monument.

But if we do nothing, they will not listen.

Goody goody

You don't have to be long at this job to recognise her sort: the caring neighbour, the bleeding heart. Curtain-twitcher, more like. Brain stuffed with shredding from the *Guardian*. You can spot them a mile off by their bohemian drapes (I mean what's off the shoulder, not in the window). Sort of scruffy chic, dressing down with loose change from the trust fund.

Still, I had to hear her out.

It was concern, she said, she didn't want to break up the family "such as it was", she didn't want the kiddies taken into care "necessarily". But you learn a lot, she said, from watching children play.

I asked how long they'd been acquainted. Reading between the lines I surmised that she employed the woman as an occasional cleaner. What other evidence did she have to support her allegations? After all, kids do pick things up off the telly.

"You don't let children watch that sort of programme," she said. "She confides in me, you see. She doesn't have many friends."

I told her I'd have a word. It's easy to criticise a single mum with three little ones to look after. When she made snide remarks about their diet I thought, excuse *me*, not everyone can afford organic hummus and guacamole. If food counted as abuse, our lot wouldn't have a moment's rest from one year to the next.

It was Sandy who went in the end. I was busy with the Hufton case, bloody disaster that turned out to be. When I remembered to ask her about it, Sandy said it didn't look all that bad: the kids were clothed and well fed and they didn't seem unhappy. We filed her under low concern and got on with managing the chaos.

But her nibs wasn't taking this lying down. There were men coming round, she told us, at all times of the day and night. "The little boy playing mummies and daddies tried to take his sister's knickers orf." Well, we had to take that seriously. She didn't help herself, mind, boasting about fixing their school uniforms and taking the whole gang to school on mornings when their mum was unconscious and slipping them "healthy food" on the sly, "not that they'll touch the stuff."

I spoke to Sandy about the case. We agreed it probably *was* a case, though we'd need more to go on than a neighbour's word. She looked to be enjoying her concern just that little bit too much. It's easy to be Florence Nightingale when social services step in to do the nursing.

"Please," she said, "whatever you do, don't let on that I told you. She trusts me, you see."

We looked into things and it did, in fact, prove necessary to intervene. The woman was going off the rails, couldn't cope at all.

Sandy swears she said nothing. Nor did I. It must have been obvious, though, given their acquaintance, and the whistleblower got a punch in the mouth for her troubles. Declined to press charges. All the same, I couldn't feel one hundred per cent sorry for her, with her thick lip. The bloody patronage of the woman! That's all the trouble with this country: we're still hobbled by *class*.

The carpenter's tale

My brothers thought me a fool to marry her. What did I want, at my age, with a disgraced girl and her swollen belly? Winks and lewd nudges presumed to answer *that* question.

"She has her hooks in you," said my sister, who thinks less of her sex than most men I know. "Batting her lashes at any man old and ugly enough to take pity on her."

But the girl did not behave like a fallen woman. She absorbed the scornful looks of her neighbours and caressed her belly as though it contained a precious gift. She used to visit me at my work. She enjoyed the heat of cedar when it glows from the saw and the smell of sandalwood, whose fragrant pairings she gathered like petals from the sand. Whenever I asked about the child she fended off my questions, and in time I was able to set aside the words that hurt us.

Though many years her senior (slowing, now, and in need of my assistants), there were times, at the start of our married life, when it seemed the other way round. I could not keep from grumbling as we made our way to the census, but she never complained, though the child was huge in her and beginning to descend.

When the baby came, it was agony to see them so poorly lodged. Many times I had to leave them in search of food and water – looking, always in vain, for a better place to stay. From the beginning there was something remarkable about mother and child. I have never been able to penetrate the mystery of it. Returning, I would find strangers in the doorway, brushing straw from their sandals and blinking in the sunlight. They smiled at me and bowed, but when I asked I was told that it was a courtesy commonly offered to newborns and their parents.

"You are blessed," some of the visitors said. This I knew, and the secret between mother and child lengthened and deepened, like a shadow, until I became so accustomed to it that I barely sensed it. For I have been happier than I would have dared hope. And it has not been difficult to love, as far as his strange manner will allow, the lean, thoughtful and forever questioning boy. He is devout like his mother: plain observance of the Law never seems enough for him. Only his temper worries me – how angry he can become at carelessness or cruelty. Such hot rage could get a boy into trouble. Still, to be young is to be absolute. He has plenty of time to learn to submit to the world as it is.

He is approaching manhood now. Some mutter that he is falling into bad company: sinners, Zealots say, drunkards, collaborators, even prostitutes. But I do not think he will succumb. After all, the boy was born into disgrace. He knows, so young, what I have taken a lifetime to understand.

The panic room in Eden

Gifts

To Mr Thos. White. In Bideford in Devonshir in England.
Thus:
Dear Brother, I hope you are in helth along with your familie may God be with you here the sumer is almos over the fiting also we hop on acount of the furst snoes beeng not far of and all returnt to corters whence i send you thes Lins to give you nus of ouer Batels gainst the injuns alas Mr Furst is kilt rid over by a hors Gorge is shot through the leg ouer regmont is struck by the Feaver but God allmity heard my prars and brot me clear it is terible this damp heet and the long wates then sodden Minuets of kiling now for the perteklers the injuns siding with the french surrunded ouer Fort on acount of the queins men refusing to pay for ther frendship i was on gard at the salley port and saw the Savages they had no hop of taking ouer Fort beeng few in number wat straunge creturs they did look Gorge was afeart at the site of them and ther songs he did ax God for delivrans but i trusted ouer sords and Cannon the shawknee delawar and Mingoe are vary ferce they took 6 forts west of the mountans and kilt many hundrets of settlers men wimin and children i thot of my Mary knee high last time i saw her with thos luvly ringlets her fingers in her mowth waving farwel by the watter medow and my Dear Wife weping to see me depart whiles we looked to the wooned so many i hope never to see such agen and how are my boys Jams must be 8 and Samul has he ridden the hors yet he was alays afeart of it I pray they never march in frunt of rogmonts of french tho it be his Magisty commands it but to return to the seege some of ouer solders were hot for batel but ofescers thot otherwise the seege did last thorough the sumer whils we a wated releef Col Henry Boucket came and saw off the enemy not withot 50 ded I haf heard say yet the Varmin were routed we gav three housays when the scotch and Royal Americans enterd no man can gues the Joy of it Captain Ekoyer gav each man a quart of rum and when i had drunk of it and watched the moon shin on the river i did think of all I have seen these years and the injuries suffert William Figors with his head shot of a girl not Marys age crusht by cannon bols what past between us Brother is no great matter i know she loved

you beter i have ben dif and blind but God has herd my prars and placed forgivenes in my hart and it is my dayly hope that I may life to come home and see you and my own Wife who is good for all that and giue her my Deuty as also to you from your most loveing Brother
Edward White

do not beleve we slept under seege the Savages are covetous and as we had three Men with the small pocks it was an easy matter to make them gifts of blankets and hankerchefs dipt in the pock woonds and in this manner did we inoculate them and God deliver us from their inhuman Nation

The monumental achievement of José Rodrigues do Cabo

Plate 1.   The only known portrait of José Rodrigues do Cabo, in 1772, shortly after his graduation from the University of Coimbra. Already a passionate naturalist, he insisted on posing with the marmoset which his uncle had brought back from his plantation.

Plate 2.   Queen Maria I of Portugal. Her concern about the exhaustion of gold deposits in Mato Grosso was reason enough to commission what would turn out to be a nine-year expedition.

Plate 3.   A sketch of the boat used on the expedition down the Rio Negro. The Indians laboured and slept in the prow, the explorers sheltered under the roof of palm leaves or *falcas*. Here, do Cabo paints while the expedition commander, Agostinho Ferreira, is cleaning his rifle.

Plate 4.   Do Cabo's portrait of a Maua Indian. In a private letter to Captain Ferreira, Queen Maria made plain her indifference to the fate of uncooperative Indians who got in the way of the expedition.

Plate 5.   A juvenile caiman: "a fierce and greedy beast, from whose carapace our shells rebound without effect." This was one of the few paintings to be left in the Real Museu by Napoleon's agents.

Plate 6.   The white-lipped peccary, *Tayassu albirostris*. "Although they make most excellent eating," wrote do Cabo in his diary, "the Indians never kill more than will support them through the rainy season." Peccaries can also be dangerous to humans. It was one of these which, in 1789, charged do Cabo and injured him in the right leg. He was compelled to use a walking stick for the rest of his life.

Plate 7.   "The Piranha," wrote Ferreira in his last letter home, "has sharp teeth and a relentless appetite. I have seen them strip the flesh from living creatures and find no satiety until the bones were clean. Everything in this place is greedy and eating seems the only law, so that I long for the quiet of civilisation." Captain Ferreira was not as forthcoming as he might have been: Do Cabo, for his part, never forgot the horrible death of the two Guaraní children.

Plate 8. It was on a slave ship like this one, plying the route between Brazil and Benin, that do Cabo, the only survivor of his expedition, began the perilous, nine-month journey back to Lisbon.

Plate 9. Matamata turtle, *Chelus fimbratus*. The shell survived in the care of the University of Coimbra, from whose meagre supply of specimens the dying do Cabo attempted to restore a collection which he believed lost for ever.

Plate 10. The naturalist Philippe Marie Saint-Hubert in 1808, shortly after returning from Portugal with do Cabo's paintings as loot. Saint-Hubert was subsequently elected a member of the French Academy of Sciences and awarded the Cross of the Legion of Honour. He is most famous today for having been that rarest of creatures: a French vegetarian.

Pileup

Nobody was responsible: it was up to everybody else to make an effort. Jim did the vacuuming. Eleanor was always cleaning other people's hairs from the shower. Neena protested that she already had the care of the vegetable garden: a garden which, Nick pointed out, only Neena was interested in, the rest of the house being quite content with a patch of weeds.

"Well I'm not doing your bloody dishes," Neena said. "As a vegetarian I can't be expected to touch animal fats."

So the contest in squalor began. Jim's fry-ups adhered to Neena's vegetarian stews; Nick's ready meals rubbed against Eleanor's low-fat concoctions. For a few days they had at least the self-interest to wash the pots and cooking utensils. But the mutual affront of the pileup in the sink – a pileup that soon spread across the other surfaces of the kitchen – became such that even this consensus failed. When someone left the oven dish fouled, others retaliated by leaving the frying pan filmed with grease and the cooking pots ringed with tomato soup. Getting up at different times for different lectures, the housemates raced each other for the use of the remaining cereal bowls. Eleanor's toaster, formerly a common asset, was requisitioned by its owner.

The smell began to find them in their beds. It was sickly sweet, with currents of egg and oyster and mulch of coffee bean. Meeting in the stairs, the housemates could no longer look one another in the eye, as though the smell were some intimate betrayal of their bodies.

At last the crisis brought them together and a course of action was agreed. They locked the door to the kitchen. They would live on takeaways and sandwiches from the deli. At night they listened as matter shifted downstairs. Things stirred, they creaked and settled. Nobody dared investigate for fear of what might crawl out: bloated slugs, or strangely evolving rodents. The boys coped better with the suspense than the girls. Neena found herself a boyfriend and spent her nights in college. When Eleanor developed a rash of acne, she called in a professional cleaner.

The cleaner was a fat, sardonic West-Indian. Eleanor and the others imagined themselves hiding behind her ample figure as she unlocked the kitchen door. The smell that greeted them was of corpses. The cleaner took one look and fled.

No doubt she reported them to the council. The housemates hid from the gloved, toxic-suited experts as the kitchen – its contents and furnishings – tumbled into the skip. The cost of the cleanup was ruinous: a great slice of their loans consumed. Penniless, on rumbling stomachs, they looked with new eyes at the patch of weeds.

The acid reef

Day 4

Ready to shoot snakebite scene when the clouds let rip. Rain like a sudden volley and AD gustily shouting "Incoming". Crew manages to protect the gear but U furious, the veins fat in his neck, throwing invective at the sky. Taking the weather personally, like a tropical Lear. Doubtless his intention.

Day 6

In break from work, go snorkelling with Alice. Buffeted by strong wind, pulled by the tide and rewarded with nasty gash in left thigh which looks even worse stained with iodine. Alice gloomy on account of the bleaching: evidence of a warming, acidifying sea. Dead, brittle fans like desiccated lungs, other corals overrun with algae. Return to find U screaming at the cooks. Have to intervene. The crew is one thing, attacking our hosts another. An indulgence we cannot afford.

Day 7

Swiss documentary team arrives. Sit under parasol, swatting flies and talking about the film, the Mesoamerican reef, the difficulties of location shooting. Advise the director, a slip of a girl crushed by the heat, to take a panning shot from the well – best place to capture the line where jungle and beach meet, the Caribbean beyond. U, who has dreaded washing in the estuary for fear of crocodiles, obliges the documentary crew with footage of him wading, patting the water like a child at play.

Day 11

U impossible today. Picks fight with D who looked at him the wrong way. Have to mediate between them while simultaneously answering J's questions about the set. Am bent over plans when sudden silence from U. He is seated beneath a seagrape with an Indian child, a girl of six or seven, who has brought her parrot chick for him to admire. U enchanted by the bald, lice-infested bird, his expression beatific, the girl happy and smiling. Realise the documentary crew is recording the scene for posterity.

Day 14

Wake up with full bladder. The rain has hatched countless mosquitoes which lock on to me like heat-seeking missiles the moment I step out for a piss. A day of troubles follows: trees felled by the storm, wrecking continuity; sand flies harvesting bits of my crew to feed to their young; communal dysentery due to discontent of the cooks (M swears we ate rancid turtle last night; Alice, due for a close-up, pukes everything up for the ghost crabs to pick over). Yet I could cope with these were it not for the worsening behaviour of U.

Day 17

The documentary crew has gone. Recall U telling them about the jungle: how he feels at home in it, restored to his true self. This is of course nonsense. U hates the jungle and everything that lives in it – demanding that vegetation be cleared twenty metres from his (air-conditioned) tent, to keep – his words – the *filthy wildlife* from crawling near. When he fails to get his way, U shouts at the crew, his fellow actors and, worst of all, the Indians, whom in the film his character rescues from cruel missionaries. I watch the fear he creates in their eyes; the natives never raise their voices in anger.

Day 22

For third day, U refuses to emerge from his tent.

Day 23

U screaming in the night as if a snake has just bitten him. Medic is allowed into his tent. The problem? U cannot sleep, demands a sleeping pill. "Give him a hundred," mutters D.

Day 25

The big scene with all the Indians in battledress finally in the can. U remarkable throughout: his performance searing the lens, eating up the scenery so that we will see nothing but his rolling eyes. Am delighted with him – until he starts to scream at the interpreter, those same eyes popping out of his terrible face.

Day 26

Ten days over schedule and I don't want to know how far over budget. For having reprimanded U over his hysterics, we have Achilles once more sulking in his tent.

Day 29

More of this shit.

Day 31

Alice airlifted to Managua. We gather about the satellite phone for news of her condition. All of us, that is, save U.

Day 42

Almost done at last, though close to the end of my strength and sanity. This afternoon, when they ought to be sleeping (only *we* are crazy enough to work in the heat), I receive a delegation from our hosts and welcome them into my tent. Very quietly and with utmost politeness they offer to kill U on my behalf. I send them away with thanks and cautious language. For tonight at least, I will allow myself the luxury of contemplating taking them up on their kind offer.

From a dictionary of slang, circa 2050

Aprust *n.* the name commonly given to April, for its resemblance to August.

Barclays (Bank) *n. British* a native of the USA, **Yank**. A piece of rhyming slang used by insurgents of the London Underground in the 2040s. *"The Barclays came and torched the place."* (New York Times, 10 March 2042)

broad, broadster *n. British* a refugee from the flooded counties of East Anglia. The term is derived from the former Norfolk Broads. For East Anglians, see also **bloater, flounder, jellyfish, wader** and **webfoot**.

carboid *n.* a foolish person, a social nuisance. Elision of "carbon" and "android": literally, a carbon-spewing android.

dubbya *n. American* an irresponsible and incompetent boss: someone promoted above their abilities. Also denotes someone with a poor grasp of reality.

goo-packer *n. British* anyone working in nanotechnology. Probably derived from the term coined by Eric Drexler (1986) to describe the hypothetical threat from self-replicating molecular nanotechnology.

green zone *n.* a delusional state of mind; the confusion inhabited by recovering alcoholics.

hornbill *n.* an excessive user of nanocaine. The term refers to the artificial septum available online for those wishing to avoid the questions of a plastic surgeon.

hubbert *vb* to stockpile provisions in expectation of societal breakdown. Etymology disputed.

ice-capper *n. American* a doomed attempt to redeem a hopeless situation. *"Putting Sendecki to bat, at this stage in the game, is a total ice-capper."* (US TV sports commentary, 2046)

Janril *n.* a name commonly given to January, for its resemblance to April.

limpet *vb British* to stay put, obstinately, in spite of disaster. *"I made up my mind to limpet until the last roof in Lowestoft sank beneath the waves".* (The Times, 19 October 2049)

mercurial *adj.* of someone who obsessively monitors the thermometer.

pumped *adj. British* defunct, utterly exhausted. Usually to describe a state of mind or body. The word derives from the failure of the Greenland Pump in the middle of the century.

quality time *n. American* torture, as in "spending quality time" with someone. The expression was restricted to military slang but has spread into popular usage, notably as a niche term on pornographic websites.

shanty *adj. British* intrusive, unwelcome, pushy. Derogatory origins: a shanty town dweller.

shruggle *n.* grudging acceptance of a hateful necessity. *"The Schultz/Hideki plan to rebuild the city on rafts met with a resounding shruggle." (Guardian*, 28 February 2038)

towner *n. British* abbreviated: shanty town dweller, a refugee. Originally specific to the Surrey Hills and North Downs.

trashware *n.* **1.** *American* the fashion for accumulating technological gadgetry under the skin. **2.** *World Standard English* contraband trade in human organs, implicitly of dubious quality and/or provenance.

umbrellaphant *n. Irish* a person who, by staying under shelter to avoid the weather, has grown extremely fat.

Vera *n. British* a girl or woman addicted to virtual reality, or VR. Subsequently, the term has been extended to anybody who attempts to escape the relentless horror of contemporary life.

Yangtze fish *n. Australian* oxymoron, a contradiction in terms.

The panic room in Eden

They had a right to be well: he had *paid* for it. You don't spend thirty million on a state-of-the-art terrarium without securing guarantees on your investment. But Milton had been trying to get through to Biosphere for days and no one was answering. Someone up there would be working on it, he said, to reassure his loved ones. Meanwhile they would have to live without the power shower.

He had always believed in providing for his family. Theirs had been the first terrarium on the block (the neighbours had driven over to look) and he had stinted on nothing, buying Paradiso air-con, water generators, a two-acre automated Crop-o-Sphere, landscape simulators, a sick bay, a panic room complete with VR play den for the kids, even a polymerised garden for his wife; all of it plugged into the benign and ineffable mind of the central computer.

Milton looked through the window at his kids in their visors. Today they were being taught history by Ronald Reagan. He turned on the sprinklers in the leisure garden to give the plants that living, after-rain look. Not that his wife would appreciate it. Milton worried that she was getting morbid. Also she was overeating – something they could ill afford. Still, it was with a sense of pride that he patrolled, as every morning, the fastness of their shelter. He checked that everything was in working order; he tried not to think, as he passed the swing he had rescued from their burning garden in Phoenix, of their eldest daughter who had lost faith.

Why had she risked it? Why go back to all *that* when they had everything they could possibly need right here? Milton followed his usual route to the Crop-o-Sphere and inspected his tomato plants in their yellow polythene sacks. She had forsaken her family. And his wife acted so understanding, though she'd stayed in bed for a week and wept over it.

Well, *he* hadn't the luxury of such emotions. He had read all the booklets that came with the terrarium, and followed the instructions on keeping cheerful.

Milton pinched one of the tomatoes. It burst and dribbled over his fingers. He did the same with others that looked fine on the surface.

All were rotting on the stalk. With a brackish taste of fear in his mouth, he walked through the squash and pumpkin patch, spying everywhere the signs of infection.

The phone was still dead. Milton could hear excessive laughter from his wife's bedroom where he had left her watching old, studio-shot comedies (anything with outdoor scenes would make her howl). An hour or so later, as the day lights began to fade, Milton returned to the Crop-o-Sphere armed with a rake, a spade and a trowel.

In the panic room, his children had dismissed the ancient President and were running beneath their visors through the lush green fields of fairyland.

Stills from the Anthropocene Era

1.
For Christmas
this year
a bumblebee.

2.
Twitchers
watching egrets
on Hackney Marsh.

3.
Sheltering from smog
in a shopping mall
reading Li Po.

4.
A guillemot feeding
its young
to the sea.

5.
A Scotch argus
running out
of mountain.

6.
A bricklayer
stripped to the waist
on Halloween.

7.
Makers of SUVs
preparing emergency
discounts.

8.
Quixotic locals
tilting at
wind farms.

9.
Clerics imploring
rival gods
above a dry well.

10.
A forest fire
extinguished
by floods.

11.
God's blessing
on both sides
in a war over water.

12.
Farmers protesting
outside a golf course
in Nevada.

13.
Environment ministers
arriving in Perth
by private jet.

14.
Beautiful women
sipping champagne
at an arms fair.

15.
A child
returning from school
quaking with fury.

16.
A cottage garden
prospering still
in photographs.

17.
A benefit concert
for the displaced people
of Norfolk.

18.
Men in suits
shaking their heads
over Africa.

19.
The hump of a bridge
becoming
an island.

20.
Getting to the opera
in Covent Garden
by boat.

21.
Wives of statesmen
enjoying a cruise
to the North Pole.

22.
Shanty towns
spreading across
the Surrey Hills.

23.
Six people
to one room
in a second home.

24.
A conversation
between Parliament
and a limpet.

25.
A mother
describing snow
to a listless child.

26.
Masking the smell
of rotting mammoth
in the tundra.

27.
A refugee camp
on the bed
of Lake Baikal.

28.
The armed invasion
of the Amazon
by US special forces.

29.
Political prisoners
planting trees
on Ellesmere Island.

30.
Amsterdam
resurgent
on stilts.

31.
A founder member
of the Spitsbergen
Seed Bank.

32.
The President cancelling
her predecessor's
mission to Mars.

33.
Worshippers
at the Temple
of Blessed Gaia.

34.
Police disrupting
forbidden rites
of propitiation.

35.
Anthropophagi
photographed in
Yokohama.

36.
The Australian Cabinet
in its new quarters
on Antarctica.

37.
Collateral damage
after the siege
of Kirkuk.

38.
Zionists celebrate
the rebuilding of
the Temple of Solomon.

39.
Victims of
the terror-famine
in Brest Litovsk.

40.
Palestinians celebrate
the destruction of
the Temple of Solomon.

41.
"Proof of life"
in deep space
declared a fake.

42.
Subcontinent
officially
uninhabitable.

43.
The last recorded
performance of
Hamlet.

44.
The US President
announcing
The Rapture.

45.
The moon
high and dry
looking on, looking on.

Visitors Book

we had a wonderful time I loved the trees and the wood ants alek saw a red squirral but I was to slow please bring back the beaver and the links they are part of the balance of Nature

Katy

A most memorable visit! The Caledonian forest is a marvel and Mr Muir a most instructive guide! Highly recommended!

Robert and Wilma Dalrymple

I never knew it was so rich: birches and willow and alders and Scots pine. How lovely, despite the midges! Shocking to think only 1 per cent of it survives. I will certainly come back to the Caledonian forest – maybe see a black grouse lek next time, who knows?

Margaret from Govan

A beautiful place. We should all love trees and destroying them so we can wipe our bums is just insane?! Alec, you really made me think. Next time I will take the train instead of flying, honest.

All best wishes,
Sandy Parnell

We have meant to come on this expedition ever since the children were old enough. Glad we made it at last. Unfortunately the guide, though courteous and informative, rather depressed everyone with his talk about the environment. We came here to recharge our batteries, not to feel like everything is doomed. Of course one can imagine the loneliness of living and working in this cottage, so far from the comforts of civilisation. Perhaps a holiday is in order?

Andrew and Mandy Harrison, Surrey

Cheer up, Alec! It may never happen!

Sunderland Tony

A wonderful location but not as warm a welcome, to be honest, as we'd hoped. The guide (or is he a hermit who keeps getting interrupted?) left us feeling ashamed of our ignorance about woodland ecology rather than illuminated. This was not what the glowing endorsements on your website led us to expect!

Ben & Celina (Ayr)

Interesting place, nice countryside, sorry we have to leave so early.
Vic and Jan Morgan

The forest is of course beautiful though the walk up was rather hard going and some steps are sorely needed. But the bothy where we stayed was dirty, unheated and full of leaves. The food was seriously below par and I did not appreciate Mr Muir's comments about our Land Rover. We did not pay to be badmouthed like this and blamed for all the ills in the world.

Mrs J. McGrath

Alec, you have a beautiful soul but you mustn't take responsibility for the whole world on your shoulders! Remember that the world is a CIRCLE and NEVER ENDING and that you are only a PART of it.

River, Santa Barbara

I am not staying here another minute to put up with this leftwing claptrap. I will be writing an official letter of complaint.

B. Slater

I am simply appalled to learn about the forthcoming closure of this bothy and the invaluable service rendered by Mr Alec Muir. Why is he not appreciated I would like to know? Perhaps because he speaks the truth about the terrible things we are doing to our planet and no wonder when he sees the seasons change out of all recognition. I have come here on holiday every year for five years and was shocked to find my host so brought down by the short-sightedness of his employers. Don't you realise what a jewel you have in your crown?

Norman Stone

*

Never will we forget the beauty of the Highlands in the fall. My family comes from these parts and it was wonderful to walk where my ancestors walked and to see the beautiful forest with its mosses and the lichens on all the trees. My husband is a Rockies man and he said it reminded him of home only it's a lot wetter! Thank you, Highland Fling, for arranging a truly unforgettable weekend. As for Alison, she is a witty, charming and enthusiastic guide: in short, irreplaceable.

Annie Chisholm
(from Santa Fe, New Mexico)

All my little ones

Tête de veau

At first glance she does not think it can be real. It looks waxy or made of latex; the colour seems wrong, pale as a human foetus and apparently as hairless. Gabriella stops on the pavement. Under the display lights, the rubbery head glistens as though from perspiration. It *has* to be false – who would display such a thing in a window with *food* in it? She sidles a little closer, a clot of nausea in her throat, and looks into the cabinet with its explicit meats: quails, plucked, with their limp heads intact, a long white tongue like some etiolated creature of the deep, rabbits with the ducts and valves of their innards exposed. Plucked birds, organs and dead rabbits she can cope with; this is Paris, after all, a city contemptuous of euphemism. But this head seems excessive to her. With a tremor of apprehension, she notices the eyelids sprigged with blonde lashes and the tufts of hair at the tips of the rigid, fleshy ears. Such efforts at verisimilitude! Then she finds another detail that would not have occurred even to the most skilful of prosthetic artists. The calf's muzzle is pressed against the Perspex of the display case. The flesh is blurry with the pressure and distorted, reminding her of the white snouts of schoolboys smudged against the windows of a sweet shop.

Dear God, it's real! A calf's head with a price tag beside it! Thin pink blood lies in pools inside the nostrils. From where she stands, Gabriella can just discern, without daring to look more closely, the raw flesh of the exposed neck and the yellow shirring of skin and fat where the blade has done its work. Her hand takes refuge between two buttons of her blouse; she can feel her brassiere and the clammy heat of her skin. Gabriella likes to think of herself as a sophisticated woman. Still, she takes the exposure of this decapitated innocent as a violent affront. The poor creature (she shudders in the midst of her fascination) cannot have seen many days before it was – what? – strung up and bled to death. Such cruelty, she thinks, such *brazenness*. What if a child should pass by? Of course, the French are inveterate carnivores. Even Sylvain would think her ridiculous for quaking in front of the facts of life. Back home, he would say, in England, where your butchers know discretion, does not every dead calf leave behind a head? Who disposes of it? What becomes of the pale and innocent flesh? Is the skull boiled down or powdered in some ingenious way, or are there landfills, just waiting for appalled archaeologists, stacked high with the heads of cattle? Gabriella's own head reels. She remembers pyres burning in English fields; the holocaust of diseased livestock; rigid hooves crumbling into smoke. But this is Paris and she is in love. Down that avenue, a hundred and forty years ago, a crowd was murdered by cannon. Not fifty yards from where she stands, in 1944, three freedom fighters were gunned down. She is in the City of Lights. She is also in Calvary, in the midst of Golgotha.

Gabriella's ankle teeters as she turns. She has forgotten about the wine she meant to buy; she passes the pharmacy, with its photographs of bronzed flesh, and does not go in for the after-sun lotion that would have soothed her sunburnt neck. She hurries back to the apartment – to her lover, to his books and music. She will not forget this casual atrocity. For a fortnight at least, until a restaurant in Islington offers calf's liver with Belgian frites, no meat will pass her lips.

Singer

Her larynx was removed when they found the tumour. The nurse couldn't figure her out, you see, whereas I know her, I understand her needs. Are you sure I can't fix you some coffee?   Well *I* sing like an old crow but she listens to music radio. Sometimes, to cheer her up, I put on her old records. I can tell from the way she reacts that she's very moved. Milk?   Yes, we came up here twenty years ago, before it got so crowded. She was a famous woman and we did nothing to dispel the notion that we were sisters. Perhaps it's a shame the old folk have been displaced by city people, but it makes things a lot easier for us, in terms of attitudes. Oh wait…   No, fine. Just thirsty. I bought one of those baby intercoms but she insists on using the bell.   I'm afraid that won't be possible. She gets distressed with people, except for Dr Stern and myself.   That? Oh it's all forgotten. Forgotten and forgiven. We're both still Christians in our way. It was a learning experience for the both of us. She made a good record in Europe and then a lot of bad ones. Maybe she wanted to get her heart broken one last time: just to see if she was capable of it. I think I can safely say now, this is her home. Yes: it looks like it's going to rain. If you're really set on driving back tonight…   I think it's the silence that gets to her most. When she has the strength to she writes me notes. She tells me she hears mice in the walls: the rustling of their paws, their high-pitched squealing. I tell her she imagines it, we bought this house together before she walked out, the walls were perfectly sound in all the years I lived alone. Well if there *were* mice I think I'd know about it.   Did you see that fork lightning? We need it for the garden.   Yes she does like the sound of rain. I believe she does. It's strange how we never talked about such ordinary things. I'll tell you, dear, the thing she's most afraid of is showing her fear. She always was a proud woman, proud and brave. You can put that in your article.   Did you know I trained as a nurse? I am a natural carer.   I remember when I was a kid, my cat disappeared. I called her name for days until my father found her under the sumacs. He said it was a brave death. You must go snarling at the enemy, he said. It makes no difference, my brother replied, while I sat trying to soothe the hackles out of my dead cat's fur. "Devotion" is a good word for it. It's hard to be loved, dear. It's good to be needed.

The kingdom upstairs

The day Lydia found out she was pregnant, a new neighbour moved in upstairs. Lydia and Tom were too preoccupied to notice.

Coming back that evening with a bottle of cordial instead of champagne, Tom observed through the banisters that the light was on in the flat upstairs. Someone was in occupancy.

It was the quiet that struck them. Their previous neighbour had caused them much grief.

Tom came back down. His name's Kevin he said. Their invitation to tea had been politely declined.

So long as he's a *quiet* loner said Lydia.

The most they heard was the creaking, at night, of floorboards above their bedroom. It wasn't pacing exactly: more the sound of shifting and pausing, of hesitation and decision.

In the bedroom they installed a cot. Tom, sweating, considered the flat-pack instructions.

I need a hex key he said. No harm in asking.

Shadows had lengthened by the time he returned. You wouldn't believe it he said. Thousands of figurines. The whole place covered. Dwarves under the bed, elves in the kitchen…

Did you get the hex key asked Lydia.

Tom went up a couple more times for small items: strong glue, a Stanley knife. He told Lydia what he'd seen, the tour he was offered among the model kingdoms. The fireplace was a cave of dragons. Goblins snickered under the kitchen units. Lydia concealed her irritation at the half-heartedness of his derision.

Several nights in a row, Tom returned late from work. On the Friday his parents-in-law came to visit, bringing baby clothes. Supper was cold by the time Tom made his entrance. He had specks of paint on his fingernails.

He's got no family said Tom.

You have.

I only helped him paint some armour.

She waited for Kevin to go out, hoping to study him through the spy-hole, but he moved fast and the most she ever caught was a glimpse of his bulk, a shaggy mane, his distant ascending profile.

After the row, Tom was careful to come home on time. He ate and then set to assembling the changing table, the storage cupboard for toys.

Lydia contemplated her bump. The little being in there. They had discovered in ultrasound the peaks and valleys, the bogs and hills in which it grew. She was a month off when Tom told her about the conference in Cardiff.

Three whole nights?

I have to go. It's my department.

Lying back to back on opposite edges of the bed, the cot in moonlight at its foot, they listened to the movements overhead.

Tom set out for Cardiff while Lydia was at the neonatal class they were meant to attend together. A perfunctory note awaited her on the fridge door.

She was alone when her waters broke. Tom's mobile was switched off, as it had been for two days.

Lydia telephoned her mother. It was all happening too quickly.

Upstairs, the floorboards gave away barely a whisper.

Intervention

Amy, bored, with her pants sticking to her and her new skirt frowzy with sweat, looked out the window and saw pink elbows, shimmering bonnets, a pair of hands tapping a steering wheel. Dad was grumbling about speed cameras and bloody swindles and Mum turned in her seat with a tin of boiled sweets. Amy sucked and gauged how soon she could get away with moaning again. But the bottleneck released them and Amy recognised of a sudden the ash trees that lined the road, the dips and summits, each with its tarn of heat, and now they were on holiday, the open windows gulping air and Amy squealing at the whoosh in her head.

"Granny is too much alone," Mum said, "she *will* be glad to see us."

"Do you suppose she'll have her batty friend with her?" said Dad, and he gave a sloping look that made Mum turn around with the Evian spray. Amy offered her face to the cooling mist and said that Mr Collins wasn't batty, he was *birdy*. "He likes birds," she explained, proud of her pun, and Dad said yes, especially old ones.

But Mr Collins was not at the cottage as Granny received them with pliers in her hand and the straw hat wonky on her head. Dad brought the suitcases in and Mum said what are you pruning?

"Not pruning," said Granny.

Amy ran into the garden to check on her cherry tree. Then she looked for the wigwam but it was not in its place. Granny heard her from the kitchen. "I'm sorry, dear. I was all on my own to set it up. Maybe your father could do it."

"But Daddy's *useless*."

Normally it was Mr Collins who set up the wigwam. The wigwam was old and leathery and it smelled, but Amy liked to gather her things inside it and besides it had belonged to Mum when she was little.

Dad sighed on the sofa and Amy went off angrily to sit in the grassy patch beside the tool shed. She sat for such a long time that seed heads left an imprint on her legs. Bored, despite having a ladybird poo in her hand, Amy got up and found Granny kneeling beside a wire cage at the bottom of the garden.

"Did Mr Collins make it?"

"No," said Granny, and she pressed her lips together so that lines appeared on her face.

"What's it for?"

Granny looked up and thought for a moment. "It's for the songbirds."

"What songbirds?"

"You're too small to know, but this place used to be full of them."

Amy pulled at the elastic in her sock. "Can Mr Collins put up my wigwam tomorrow?"

Granny bent down with her pliers to tie up some metal ends. "Forget about Mr Collins," she said and twisted the metal ends with a sharp, angry tug.

The next day Amy woke up in a room full of angled shadows. She listened for sounds of movement in the cottage and heard her father snoring. But she couldn't hear Mum and this made her bold to get up.

The downstairs curtains were closed but the ones in front of the terrace were moving in the breeze. Amy stepped outside, barefoot, and the grey sky she expected turned blue with cottony clouds. There were bumblebees and hoverflies and the grass felt wet underfoot. She was walking on the grass because of the voices coming from the bottom of the garden.

Mum was there in her pyjamas. Granny was facing her, dressed in yesterday's clothes with the hat still on her head and her hair spilling madly under its rim. "I'm not surprised he left," Mum was shrieking. "How could you do this? How could you?"

Granny shook her head, the lines hard about her mouth. Mum looked where her eyes had gone.

"Don't come here," Mum said. "Stay there, darling." But the sob choked in her voice only made Amy panic and she ignored the instruction. Mum rushed to stop her, to catch her in her arms, but it was too late to prevent her from seeing the cage, its open jaw, and the magpies lying, limp and broken, on the grass beside it.

"It's nothing, darling. Your grandmother hasn't slept all night."

"Someone has to do something," Granny said. "They kill all my little ones. They're *murderers*."

The overnighters

"It's a question of space. It's a question of, okay, we can't keep everything. I know this goes against your instincts and your training. It goes against mine, trashing books, I don't like it either. But put yourselves in my shoes for a minute. We don't have the resources to keep what we have and accommodate future titles. It's like the world, you know, people have to die to make room for new people. So it's the same for us. It's making room for the next generation."

"It's the next generation we have in mind," Lol said to Tony over a Skinny Latte. "Think of the Iroquois."

"The Iroquois didn't use libraries."

"They asked what impact their actions would have in seven generations. Kastner doesn't understand like legacy. He's management, he's about the bottom line."

"Look for a loophole," said Geena. "That's what lawyers do when the law's fixed. You look for the loophole."

Tony and Lol and Geena read through Kastner's letter. Their three heads – balding grey, dyed red, straightened black – met above the paper and their identity passes almost touched in the air. Geena was the first to move away. She picked up her Tazo® Chai and Lol watched her.

"You found a loophole?"

"No but I found a cheat."

"I'm not doing anything illegal," said Tony.

"What it is is, we got a way of preserving the collection. We don't have to break the law. Jeez Tone, you're so paranoid."

"I'm careful is all."

Geena put on her glasses. "What the basis is for trashing titles is how long a book has gone without a request. Anything that hasn't been called up in five years is for landfill. Okay, so this is a dumb-ass way to evaluate the value of a book. But knowing the rules means knowing how to make them work for us."

Lol and Tony listened as Geena thought out their strategy. It would mean staying late. Lol didn't mind about the nights as her kids were in college and she had no one home since Norm passed. Geena's mom would be only too happy to look after Leticia.

"Tony?"

"I think it's a crazy notion."

But Lol and Geena were already grinning at the prospect of their mission. Tony shook his head and went to buy another cup of Zen™.

*

Tony was walking in the park beside the river. It was a warm night. The air was spiced. Sprinklers and cicadas rhymed. He sighed like the one responsible adult and turned around.

He found the library in darkness; let himself in with his staff key. He saw headlamps, like miners had just surged up from under ground. Lol and Geena were going through the shelves, picking up volumes and checking the borrowing slips. "This one's *never* been taken out." "This book's waited since 2000." Anything that was due for elimination got a date pencilled in: a new lease of life!

Lol giggled. "This is, like, Geena's List."

Tony got given a hand-torch and he took it to the small philosophy section. That night the books he saved included *The Philosophy of Beekeeping* by Merle Beckstein, *Uncommon Moths of the Western Palaearctic*, *Quaker Quilts* (14 illustrations, b&w) and *Incantations of the Hopi Indians* by Frances Blue Jay Wilson.

They converged in the foyer at three am. "Well that's a start," Geena said. Tony wished his colleagues goodnight or good morning and left the building.

He walked home beneath the stars.

Thank Christ they hadn't yet moved to the IT database. That would mean changing the call-up dates *on computer*. Geena was smart and Lol was sassy but neither of them would make a good hacker. Tony could, but that was for something entirely different, and he wasn't going to confess to any of *that* stuff anytime soon.

Dormeus

what is that tapping sound, i'm not imagining it, i'm certainly not *dreaming*, chance would be a fine thing, where is it coming from and why must i be alone to listen to it, i should hear nothing, i should fear nothing, like my relatives all curled up in sleep, whole months of it, oblivious to wind and rain, to the rime that coarsens the leaves, to that tapping sound, is it coming closer, is it something hungry crawling on its belly towards hot blood, i say hot, their hearts are barely beating while mine pounds in my chest, could it be that tapping sound is *me*, is it my heart, i've made the mistake before, like chasing your own tail, oh, if only we had stayed up there, in the hollow, holed up, but my kin are creatures of habit, they gathered the bark as usual, they gathered the grass as usual and the moss, what comforting industry before the great slumber, working up an appetite for it, i'm as hungry as the rest of them but the feast is not for me, i listen to them gorging on it, there's nothing like six months of unconsciousness to dull the edge of terror, if at least they knew what i did for them, what a service i render, keeping vigil, listening out for danger, not that it can help much, they're all so fat on sleep, even in summer when the flowers are gone and you're lucky to have a grub to chew on they sink into a torpor, a snout will cast its shadow, the jaws close over a dream and you wake up in someone's gullet, but enough of that, I must not think of that, though I will have to sooner or later, this sitting here is all very well and it's warm enough if you don't mind the occasional shiver but everything that lives must eat, it's the LAW, i'm perishing here, the fat is melting off me, if only i could be like the rest of them, but i've run out of strategies, there aren't enough sides of my body to lie on, i've never seen a sheep, so i convince myself that they need me, that this torment serves a purpose, for someone has to keep an ear twitching, complacent oafs, but they're not to blame they're just doing what comes naturally, what ought to come naturally, am i unnatural then, a false start and a dead end, who will want to breed with me come spring, i'll be a wreck, all skin and bones, they won't know what i did for them, they won't have heard the tapping, it's coming from outside, i can hear breathing, i can feel vibrations in the soil, i'm not alone in being hungry, there are no haws no sloes no nuts no berries, no point in staying put, i'll only use up my store of fat, my supply of heartbeats, can it be worse than this, it will only last an instant, oh my kin, my companions, think of me when you come round, and do not mourn, not that you would, for i am gone to meet the great sleep that is the goal of all our slumbers and has the added kindness of being without dreams

Wild things

Mr Gillespie was not a friend to wilderness. In its proper place, of course, it was all very nice, he had nothing against wilderness per se. But it had no place in a garden. Driving his wife home from the hospice, Mr Gillespie used to shake his head at gardens where the grass had grown to seed or trees sprawled and ivy crept up the walls of houses. Letting things go like that – allowing nettles to swamp a flowerbed, or ignoring the spread of goose-grass till it plucked at the heads of flowers and dragged them down to its level – were derelictions of neighbourly duty.

Of course, in an age of ASBOs and yobbos, it was hardly surprising that the art of lawn care should be in decline. But Mr Gillespie, as his wife faded before his eyes, never neglected their own garden. Even in the last weeks, when she was in the hospital, he occupied his time away from her with keeping down the grass and cutting back the growths on her espaliered apple trees.

No one, peering over the garden fence, could have called the Gillespies neglectful people. No one could have pretended that they weren't good neighbours.

Mr Gillespie buried his wife on the first hot day of the year. They had no children but her sister came from Cornwall, as did colleagues from work. Standing above her grave, Mr Gillespie noticed what he thought was smoke but was in fact pollen from a parasol pine. He drove home and, in spite of the heat, locked all the doors and windows.

That first spring, the lawn got out of hand. Dandelions sprouted and nobody uprooted them; docks and shepherd's purse wriggled above the tall unmannered grass. But Mr Gillespie had not gone to ground. He would emerge as usual to go to work or to buy food, always using the front door while the door to the garden stayed locked and the curtains never parted in the rear windows.

A blazing summer turned the nation's lawns to straw but not the grass in Mr Gillespie's plot. The dense blades shielded the ground from the heat of the sun, and it was only as seed heads ripened that his garden turned the tawny colour of a meadow in July. Other plants escaped their restraints and began to spread. The disciplined apple trees produced new branches while the lilac thickened and an elder, carried in the bowels of a visiting blackbird, began to work its way out of the shade.

In the autumn, apples fell of their own ripeness and wasps became drunk on their rough cider. Then winter came and things died back, or consolidated the ground they had stolen. Mr Gillespie withdrew from sight, going about his business in the early hours of the morning. Meanwhile the plot he had tamed for his wife continued to change without him.

A second spring came and the lilac blossomed while clematis sprawled over from a neighbour's garden. Nettles began to creep under the fence and a firethorn erupted, unbidden. Older residents looked at the apple trees that were breaking their bonds and, later in the year, at the blowsy apples and the dense grass, and they shook their heads as though at some betrayal, a display of grief spilling over into chaos.

Autumn returned with the moaning of leaf blowers, then winter and a third spring, and still nobody took as much as a stick to Mr Gillespie's jungle. Some said the man had lost his wits. Others complained about the disorder and blamed him for the weeds in their own flowerbeds. Over the summer holidays, children gathered on the decking of parental gardens, among patio heaters and palm trees, and plotted to climb the rotting fence into the patch of wilderness.

That first time, Mr Gillespie heard them whisper and laugh. The children waded in the long grass and Mr Gillespie opened a window without drawing back the curtain. He sat in the wicker chair chosen by his wife and leaned on his open palm, listening to the children playing. The children returned to the garden several times and each time he was surprised by his readiness to accept them. Indeed, it got so that he longed for the sound of their voices.

Cooler weather came and he listened and listened, unaware that their games had taken them elsewhere. Eventually, lured by the soft music of rain on leaves and troubled by the absence of children, Mr Gillespie sought out a key and opened the patio door.

A few pot plants had died of neglect but this was made up for by the profusion of weeds muscling through the cracks in the paving.

Rosebay willowherb had colonised the terrace, as it had the bombsites of his childhood in Coventry. He looked at a clot of orange and black caterpillars wound about a flowering ragwort. He saw the rank and overgrown plot – the flock of goldfinches feeding on the seed heads of teasel, the *chip-chip* alarm call of a blackbird that had been feeding on the lilac's fruit. He descended the mossy steps and launched into the tangled garden. Everywhere, things had slipped their boundaries. He made his way past hogweed and cow parsley to the once espaliered apple trees, where he sat down in the long grass and looked towards the blind and shuttered house. The garden had become a wilderness. And Mr Gillespie saw that it was good.

Bog man

When they started out he shouted in triumph like a boy returning from battle. People who had known him lined the route bearing garlands of flowers and tossing before his feet, and the feet of his two companions, broken eggshells. The shards stung and adhered to his flesh: save for the cap fastened under his chin and the hide belt around his waist, he was naked.

It pleased him, in the breadth and dazzle of dawn, to feel the eyes of women on his body. Daylight explored him; the dye on his skin gripped and cracked under the wind's scrutiny. On the margins of the settlement he heard keening from within a hut, though his eyes, which rolled and stared like those of a running horse, took in only the branches of rowan and whitethorn that blazed outside the gate. Dimly amid the tumult of his brain he recalled that one very like himself had dreaded this part of the journey; but that was before his fast and purification, before the bonfires that scoured the darkness and the bitter broth, offered at sunrise, whose mixture of barley and linseed, knotweed and bristlegrass had scorched the dread out of his limbs and set his mind blazing towards its consummation.

The escorts watched him closely. His bride was waiting, they said. The naked man looked down at his erection and laughed and did not think to wipe the spittle from his lips.

It was necessary, as they negotiated a path through ash trees, for the men to assist him. The trees thinned and dwindled, the plain levelled out, and for the first time they felt a twinge of resistance in the shivering, painted body.

"Courage," said one of them. "This is what you were born for."

Smoke clung to the surface of the bog; it had drifted down from the hillsides where, yesternight, cattle had been driven between two fires. His escorts spoke to him about the summer that was coming: it would blow these shadows from the sweet earth, they said, his brothers would lead their livestock out to pasture and he would be with them, every blade of grass his gift.

The naked man looked at his hands. They were clean and unblemished. His body had the softness of one who has been spared toil.

The others understood the work of the broth. Visions of loveliness, even now, would be dancing before the man's eyes. They guided him through moss and heather, one implacable hand under each of his armpits. The naked man began to gibber; his arms and legs burned, great pains tore up his belly. He crouched into the bog to vomit.

The strong men raised and supported him to the place where water gushed clear and cold from a fissure in the moss. Around the water's tongue the plants grew whose seeds he had eaten that morning.

The naked man stood, legs half bent, like a child exposed to frost, and his roiling eyes seemed to recognise the place. Unsupported, he fell again and attempted to haul himself away from the spring. The sphagnum moss seemed to suck him down, the goddess pulling him already into her. He fought off, with a strength that surprised his assailants, their first attempt to sling the rope about his neck. The men persisted: his delirium was too far gone for persuasion. Besides, they knew it was often thus. They redoubled their efforts without anger or malice. It was no sacrifice if it cost nothing. The man had to die so that others might live.

Orpheus's lot

Orpheus's lot

Orpheus? It certainly rings a bell. I get so many, you know – impossible to keep track of every one. You'd think that was the advantage of this job, you get to meet all sorts: peasants, kings, adulterous wives, murdered husbands, warriors, philosophers – you name it, I've had them in the back of my boat. But to be honest, and I always am honest, most of them are a major disappointment. All that moaning, all that special pleading. You'd think they'd show a *bit* of dignity. Philosophers are the worst: half of them say they don't believe in you, the other half can't stop asking questions. And you'd never *imagine* the number of people who seem to reckon the rules shouldn't apply to them. Actors, for instance: so they made people laugh, they dished up a bit of pity and fear – it's no reason to expect special favours. How about yourself, sir? Lost your head, I see. Well, it's more original than many. I've had a city's worth of plague victims lately. It gets monotonous.

Sleep? No, I don't go in for that sort of thing. No Time, for starters. Except once, and that was unfair. Hang about – it's coming back to me. *Orpheus*. He was the one who tricked me. Didn't pay his fare, either. It's as fresh as if it were yesterday. Which, as far as I'm concerned, it was. Curly hair, lovely singing voice. Charmed wild animals, made trees and rocks dance, even diverted the course of rivers. Could have made a lot of money with a talent like that. He just started plucking his lyre and before I knew it, bam, I'd nodded off and he'd hitched a crossing.

It was a love thing. Eurydice was the name. Snakebites, if I remember. Blighter had balls, I'll give him that – not since Hercules came down and bashed the mutt about did anyone living try and pull *that* trick. And his methods were subtler. He softened my boss's heart, which I have to admit was impressive. Or I should say: the music worked wonders on his wife. She's always been the softie of the two. Human, you see: you never shake it off. And the boss is devoted to her, believe it or not, so when Orpheus got her on side, it was almost inevitable. Mind you, the boss is cunning. That not looking back clause: Orpheus was bound to fall for it. The boss doesn't grant favours. Not in his nature – or his remit. And besides, it wouldn't be fair, would it? Eurydice got put back among the shades where she belonged. Everything came right in the end. You seem very interested.

It's yourself, isn't it? I recognise you now. I'm useless with names but I never forget a face. Here, you haven't got that lyre, have you? I don't want to be caught napping again. Still, no hard feelings. Sit back and enjoy the ride. You'll be staying with us a little longer, I take it, this time…

Gorgon

As far as we in the hills are concerned, the reign of the gorgon began with rumours, and I half believed them, for though the stories grew more horrible with every telling, they had the partial authority of witness. Someone had found the discarded limbs, the spilt viscera: a goatherd perhaps, stumbling across a petrified mother and the remains of her child.

This was at a time of high prices, when every merchant's thoughts were with his shipments of grain. Talk of monsters was bad for business: it made buyers cautious and kept out foreign trade. When a messenger ran, bloodied, into the city with tales of fresh horror, some called for a levy of troops to meet the enemy, but these excitable individuals were put in their place. We could not afford to waste time and treasure on hypothetical threats from unproven sources.

"If there is a gorgon," an elder said, "and I am sceptical on that point, then country folk have our sympathy. But they mustn't come to us that have ridden out plagues and sieges complaining of a local difficulty. We have enough on our plates not to worry ourselves with mythical creatures."

At first it was easy to ignore the gorgon: her victims, though ever more numerous, were unknown to us and of little significance. None can gaze on that hideous face and survive, yet it takes a strong constitution to look, not in the gorgon's eyes, but at the simple fact of her existence. Those who did, and shouted warnings in the streets, were regarded as troublemakers; it was the sort of thing our enemies would have us do. This did not prevent dreamers from thinking up impractical solutions: tinted-glass helmets, or a complex and hopeless device using blades and mirrors. Sceptics viewed such efforts with contempt; the gorgon was a natural phenomenon, they argued, and it was presumptuous to oppose a daughter of Gaia. Others conceded that her depredations might make life more uncomfortable for us and that the only solution was to build higher walls around our villas and to hire mercenaries to guard the hillsides. These things were done, and eventually the tide of refugees abated, knowing that nothing awaited them on the heights save the sharp points of cold iron.

The countryside emptied and famine stalked the city. A second hunger followed. We felt sorry for the victims, of course, but a quick death is preferable to slow starvation and besides, none of us had family in the slums. We hoped the gorgon's fury might exhaust itself there. Yet the creature returned, again and again, to ever more empty streets, and soon the serpents on her head were flicking their tongues towards our homes.

For the first time, we in the hills feel directly threatened. Some are indignant about this; others are given to weeping and prayer. Every day we must pay the mercenaries more to keep them from deserting. Naturally, those with the means are looking for ways out, but we chose our hills for the security they offered – the sea on one side, the city on the other. We are trapped in a prison of our own making. Very soon, one bright morning, we will awake to find the soldiers gone.

I look at my children and wonder which will be the more merciful: teeth or stone. That I can write these words does not make them any easier to bear.

Narcissus & the pool of mirrors

Trapped in the closed and perfect circle of his infatuation, Narcissus was not unhappy. His punishment for spurning the boy who adored him, to be enamoured beyond distraction of his own reflection in a pool, was intended to make him take his life – a million florists depended on it – yet this violent resolution had not come to pass. Nemesis watched as, day after day, the young man crouched above his image. That other, trapped in its mirror of shimmering fins, had no being, a fact that ought to have driven Narcissus mad. Yet he seemed content within the confines of his predicament, for no infidelity could threaten him, and he had only to reach down to his own flesh to move his image to ecstasy.

Nemesis, discomfited, endured the scorn of the young man who had invoked her aid. "Fat lot of use *you* turned out to be," Ameinias said. Bitterness had corrupted the unrequited lover: his skin was a morass of pustules and craters and the golden hair fell in strands from his head, as though an invisible bird were perched on his shoulder, plucking out the lining for its nest.

Nemesis considered punishing Ameinias for his effrontery; yet she too hated to see Narcissus's contentment. For three days she hid in her cave to think up a solution. When it came to her, every nymph and satyr in Boeotia shivered at the sound of her laughter.

Narcissus, waking one morning beside the pool where he knew his beloved awaited him, opened his eyes on a thousand reflective surfaces. Beaten gold and silver mirrors hung like fruit from every tree; there were bowls of water as abundant as daisies set out on the grass, and in each and every one of them Narcissus found his image perplexed, aroused and fearful. From opposing banks of the pool, Nemesis and Ameinias watched as the perfect boy ran from one reflection to another. Each was as lovely as the last; yet he could not hope to contemplate them all. He crawled from mirror to dish and back again, maddened by the thought of all that he turned his back on.

As the days and weeks passed and Narcissus found his reflection proliferating in all directions, his body began to coarsen. His bronzed flesh lost its lustre, his eyes sank into their orbits, his dark curls began to fall. Gratified beyond expectations, the lover he had spurned told everyone about the torment of Narcissus. Crowds gathered to watch as the famous youth attempted, in vain, and with ever more frantic and apish gestures, to contain in one glance every reflection of his decay. A thousand onlookers jeered while his image danced on the lenses of their eyes. Insatiable in their curiosity, they watched as Narcissus grew thin and unlovely. He could not eat or drink or sleep; when, in desperation, he attempted to spill or smash the likenesses that horrified him, the surfaces wherein his features wept redoubled in number. People remarked on his wrinkles and pouches; they passed comment on every instant of Narcissus's plight. So great was the general appetite that Ameinias, who was responsible for the spectacle, began to wish that it would cease, one way or another.

He was not disappointed. The pullulation of images had worn Narcissus to the bone; and it was in a spirit of great sorrow and satisfaction that people arrived one morning to deplore the condition of the celebrated corpse.

Preliminary report on the economics of unicorns

It has been exceedingly instructive, for our investigation into the potential of a domestically unproven industry, to learn about the economics of unicorns in Great Britain. I am indebted to Mr Giles Randolph of Unicorn Technological (UniT) for showing me around the farms, slaughterhouses and processing plants of his native Northamptonshire.

Briefly, here are my observations:

- Britain's national herd has continued to decline as imports of meat and horn from Brazil accelerate.

- There are currently 7.4 million head of unicorn in the UK, down by 4.3 per cent on the previous year.

- Attempts by environmentalists to link Brazilian imports with rainforest destruction have had little measurable effect. This bodes well for an industry of our own.

- The number of foals born decreased from a year ago as foaling rates struggle to recover from the Unicorn Spongiform Encephalopathy crisis. Starting a herd from scratch using Canadian stock would make us competitive in European markets from an early stage.

- Age and diet have a demonstrable impact on product yield, quality and utility. Only stallions and mares aged 6 and over and raised in woodland enclosures mimicking natural habitats produce horn of interest to the pharmaceutical industry. Increasing numbers of British farmers, made uncompetitive by the burden of EU welfare legislation, are turning to mature horn production. A national industry of our own need not attempt to compete in this area.

- The horn of colts and fillies, notably inferior, is yet, with coarse grain feeding, commercially valuable much sooner and at lower input costs. Applications include industrial lubricants, petroleum substitutes in hygiene products (a growth area given environmental concerns) and glue.

- Method of slaughter preferred in the UK: percussion stunning using captive bolt. Carbon dioxide asphyxiation is preferred in Halal slaughterhouses. Argon gas is gaining in popularity. The unit, once inert, is strung upside down by one hind leg on the processing line. Main arteries are severed in the neck causing exsanguination. Horn removal must follow immediately for health and safety and quality retention purposes.

- Owing to the exotic origins of European unicorns (Mr Randolph estimates that, at the time of Columbus, there were 50 million head on the eastern seaboard of America, compared to 40 million under intensive rearing today), British farming has long struggled with such climate-induced diseases as tuberculosis and pupura hemorrhagica.

- Other health problems occurring in intensive herds include labyrinthitis, pyoderma, Obstructive Pulmonary Disease, niggles, blort (rarely fatal with new antibiotics), recurrent uveitis, proxworm, hoof blight, horn wilt (an especial problem in the damp west of Scotland), horn canker, rotavirus infection, cystic mites and vertical fissures or "sandcracks" in the cloven hooves.

- Massive investment in genetic testing, spearheaded in China and Texas, promises solutions to some of the more costly ailments. The difference of climate will also need to be factored in before northern hemisphere breeds can be raised here. The success of the unicorn industry in Brazil bodes well on this last point; see forthcoming report from S.J. Sundaram and Anwar Ng.

- Retail equivalent value of UK industry: £2.8 billion. UK meat exports as percentage of production: 12.4 per cent. UK commercial slaughter: 4.365 million head (including 3.722 million colt and filly, 0.643 cull mare, stallion and gelding).

Mr Randolph of UniT was candid in his revelations concerning the declining state of the British industry. A detailed study of the failings and hindrances to profitability in the UK would benefit our own enterprise. Pending my more detailed report, here are two recommendations:

- How to counter the rising costs of feed? Research should be undertaken into the viability of palm oil derivatives and sugarcane as alternatives. Successful outcomes would boost the oil palm division of our company at a time when allegedly adverse impacts of oil palm expansion are impacting export sales.

- Possible appeal of unicorn meat to Chinese, Tamil and Eurasian sections of the domestic market. The recent Swine Riots in Kedah and Kelantan have discouraged minority groups from their usual pig-eating ways. I am assured by Mr Randolph that unicorn meat is an excellent substitute for pork, and being acceptable to all sections of society, we can hope to sell it to both Muslim and infidel stockists. A major (perhaps government sponsored?) campaign to promote unicorn might stimulate domestic demand for a product which is currently viewed as foreign, corrupt and undesirable.

Ahmad Ibrahim, London

Cut is the branch

Enter Mephostophilis in his own shape.

MEPHOSTOPHOLIS. Now, while my master entertains himself
Kissing the face that launched a thousand ships,
Let's be thick as thieves and spare your hisses:
Drop the moral noises, you are waiting
As am I for Faustus's comeuppance.
Why else would you bide this pitiless rain
If not to watch another come to grief?
You groundlings there, still reeking of your trade,
Take comfort from this warning to the wise:
For in the world there are no greater fools
Than scholars fed on books and starved of sense.
Four-and-twenty years have I served this one,
That still can dupe himself without my aid,
Calls "sweet" and "gentle" Mephostophilis
That only waits to tear him limb from limb:
The sort of intellectual, in short,
Who thinks this tragedy is somehow *mine*.
A devil sick of sin? As fish hate water!
I thrive on sin; it is my daily bread,
Manna from Earth in the deserts of Hell.
Leave paradox to angels: I am straight
As an arrow fired at an innocent.
I have no pity for you – why should you
Regard me, your enemy, as a friend
Knocked out of kindness by Heaven's fury?
One instance, if you please, to prove myself
The hateful creature that I mean to be.
List, list, O list!
We devils are as thick as flies in June:
Some dwell in throne rooms, others rectories,
I, seats of learning, where I chanced to meet
In Wittenberg two thinkers of renown,

Fellow students, though Faustus the older,
The younger born and raised to be a prince.
Difference of rank meant nothing to them;
Equals in the Republic of Learning,
They wallowed in analytical thought
And took delight in Aristotle's works.
Faustus, greedy for inhuman knowledge
Sold his soul in exchange for my service;
But he meant to share his discoveries
With an intellect equal to his own.
One noble mind alone fitted the bill.
Hamlet, his princely student, who was gone
In mourning home to bury his father
And scowl at the queen's too hasty nuptials,
Was yet ambitious to rule in Denmark;
Whence Faustus sent me with the stern command
To make Hamlet despair of narrow crowns
And return to scholarship's boundless realm.
This task I performed: appeared to the prince
In the groaning guise of his father's ghost,
Slipped him a fib about brotherly greed,
A fratricide-cum-regicide I'd cribbed
From a play, The Murder of Gonzago.
We devils must perforce be good actors
And I surpassed myself that night. Alas,
How was I to know it would end in blood?
Hamlet fell for the trick and I was forced
To impersonate his uncle at prayer
Lest the first imposture be discovered
And Faustus lose the best mind of the age.
A subtle sprite should foresee all, you say?
I follow my orders to the letter
And give men rope, but do not make the noose.
Enough exegesis: Hamlet is dead
Along with most of Elsinore's worthies
And another university wit's
Mouthing now a tale to credulous ears

That value tragedy over a farce.
Some scribbler then will set it down in verse
And actors mouth it on a stage like this.
O, I'm wise to the workings of your minds:
I shift shape but only you *look* for it.
Godlike in apprehension? Well, perhaps;
But discontent to be without pattern
You force your lives into a story's shape
And give us hooks with which to draw you in.
The constant in a devil's work is this:
Men never learn.
                      But soft – here Faustus comes;
His will is signed, all earthly pleasures spent,
Time's up, expired, he's passed his hell-by date
And I must claim him. We shall meet anon.

Glass slippers are a health hazard

"Elle souhaitait à la fois mourir et habiter à Paris." – *Madame Bovary*

If she so much as *looked* at another macaroon, she told herself, she would burst her stays. Why did they keep tempting her with sweetmeats? Was it the work of the king, who eyed her sometimes in ways that made her feel uncomfortable and insisted, too often and apropos of nothing, that he liked a woman to be *substantial*? The princess sighed and her ladies-in-waiting, like so many hens sunk in their feathers, straightened to watch her. Was her Royal Highness still feeling unwell? She performed a brief cough to prove it. Her husband was away in the provinces, opening some hospital or orphanage. She had been supposed to accompany him (people expected the courteous tilt of her beautiful head, the intimate and sidelong glances) but she had pleaded a heavy cold and was excused a tedious winter's journey. Before his departure, the prince might have enquired himself into his wife's condition; yet they rarely met in private. Acres of carpet and gilt separated their respective quarters, and besides, it was impossible to arrange a midnight assignation without summoning a dozen attendants from their beds.

The princess flattened with the heels of her palms the imagined bloating of her bodice. She stepped to the window. Each time she looked out, a crowd cheered, tossing its caps into the air and then trying not too obviously to search for them when they landed awry. It never ceased to surprise her that people had nothing better to do than press their noses against the palace gates. She made a gesture that might have been a wave or else aversion to a fly, and the people redoubled their celebrations. Slipping behind the silk curtains, she wondered who exactly was performing for whom.

One hundred clocks chimed in the palace: they resounded in canon through corridors and guardrooms and ceremonial chambers. Midday. The princess yawned and concealed her perfect teeth with her hand. She had expected marriage at such an exalted level to confer the privilege of at least *some* privacy; instead, she was perpetually scrutinised, so that she could not yield to the simplest physical need without attendance from obsequious courtiers. This led to a more intimate ailment. The princess had considered consulting the royal physician about her true complaint: the sleepless tedium of supposed felicity. But the quack was old and evil-smelling, a bewigged beetle obsessed with phlebotomy and the consistency of his patient's stool. The physician could not help her: nobody in this place could.

Feeling restless, she thought about taking a turn in the garden; but it was so cold that venturing out would only undermine her story about feeling unwell. Oh, the fibs that she lived by! At first, flush with love and luxury, she had thought nothing of the world's opinion of her. Not so that nebulous entity known to the world as The Palace, which, after several aristocratic scandals, had embraced the prospect of a union between the prince and a commoner of uncommon good looks. She had not seen, at the time, how thorough a job was done of gilding their love story in the public imagination. Even the name she took was invented for her by the royal historian. As if, in the days of her domestic servitude, she would ever have been careless enough to sit in the cinders! And that folklore about glass slippers, all stemming from a vulgar typographic error in the official proclamation. More preposterous still were the stories that circulated about her original family. Her father was still alive, thank you very much, while her stepmother had not been malicious for the pure hell of it. The truth was that there simply hadn't been enough money for three dowries and, like any ambitious woman, she had attempted to focus resources on her own daughters. The princess no longer felt inclined to forgive her stepmother for this; but she sensed it was important – for reasons that she could not have articulated – that the complexities of her former life be acknowledged by those who document such things.

Her ladies-in-waiting began to stir from their torpor. Soon it would be luncheon, followed by hours of tedium without the smallest menial task to distract her. Will Her Royal Highness play the lute or the virginal? Will she tousle the fur of a diminutive lapdog or test her fingers at embroidery? The princess sighed again and watched her arm extend towards the plate of macaroons. Happy endings are best, she decided, when they happen to other people.

The siren of May

It wasn't fancy that set him on his knees in the chapel praying for a wife. Niall was the ugliest fisherman in Crail. Back home, even widows shunned him. Only at sea did he forget his faults; and so he had stowed his boat and braved the birds of the Isle of May. Razorbills laughed at him and tammies made lewd comments but he paid them no attention. In the chapel he screwed his eyes tight and begged for a miracle.

A wiser man, with a wife and bairns at home, would have called the catch uncanny and sent it back. Niall managed to untangle the fluke and the narrow fin that ran up the spine. He fastened the creature to the bottom of the boat, where it foamed and wailed and wrenched at the tangles of its hair. He reached overboard with his slops bucket and heaved gallons of water into the boat. The creature quieted a little: the bilge seemed to calm it.

Niall studied the mermaid. There was something catlike about the large eyes and their slanting pupils. He regretted the lack of lashes, and he shivered when a membrane clicked across the jelly of her eyeballs. Still, she was female; her breasts were heavy, the aureoles a greenish tinge. Contemplating them and the swelling of her hips where they fused with her tail, Niall searched himself for desire. Here was this marvel, an answer maybe to his prayers. Who was he to refuse the offering?

Fishermen eyed him as he came and went on the harbour front with buckets of sea water, with limpets and whelks and bundles of dulse. Try as he might, he could not make his captive eat. She sprawled in the bathtub like a landed fish. He talked of love but she mewled and cried, and Niall could make no sense of her salty blether.

Having worried about the noises she used to make and what his landlady might think, it got so that Niall longed for a yelp. But weakness put paid to the mermaid's skirling. She would flop limply over the edge of the bath, her claws twitching in a way that reminded Niall of the foamy threshing of a landed crab. Coming with buckets of harbour water, he could not help scowling at the stink. He tried to dampen her torso, which was blizzened with lesions and blobs, and attempted to tuck the rotting edges of her fluke back into the bathwater. Previously, whenever he touched her, she would flinch and mutter; but now she was as silent as a fish, the black globules of her eyes fixed and fathomless.

He no longer worked for pay. He put out his nets for small fry: anything that might tempt his selkie-wife to live.

Her tail began to shrivel. Niall feared he would throw from the skelbs that scaled the rim of the bathtub and tinier flecks in the swats of the water. He decided to empty the lot, to start afresh as with clean linen. Within a day, the new water was barming over.

Niall wept that night over his tatties. He felt sick with shame. Though the mermaid's face had turned plucky and cankered, he was the festering one. He gagged at the sight and smell of her. Oh, she was dying! Breathless, he ran to the harbour to fetch his oilskin. His heart tholed as he turned the key in the lock. Would he find a corpse in his bath? The passage of a candle above her eyes brought the membrane slithering over.

Niall paid no attention to her weeping sores. He felt a ligament tear in his back as he heaved the mermaid onto the oilskin. In agony, he dragged the heavy burden down the stairs, past Mrs Campbell's room where the old hag was in her cups. It being early of a Sunday, there was no one about to watch him struggle with the mute and stinking bundle.

The sun was not yet up on the harbour when Niall set down his burden. He opened the oilskin with a grimace, like a boy peering into the crust of a wound. Her torso was pale, the fluke as dry as old leather. He flipped her over towards the water; the weight fell away and a plop, obscene and furtive, crawled about the harbour walls.

Niall looked down; and it was impossible to tell, in the half light, whether the tail in the water kicked or merely turned over with the momentum of its fall.

Pearly Gates tick box survey

Welcome! To help us ensure you receive the service you deserve, please fill in the following survey by ticking the boxes that apply to you.

Did you, in the course of your temporal existence, achieve or do any of the following?

Enjoy luxury for less ☐

Practise yoga in the sunset ☐

Build a snow cave ☐

Undergo a master cleanse ☐

Swim naked in a river ☐

Make love on a beach ☐

Pamper yourself on a spa break ☐

Keep a dog in a handbag ☐

Find the dress that changed your life ☐

Shake hands with royalty ☐

Blow a month's wages on shoes ☐

Get married in Vegas ☐

Get remarried in Vegas ☐

Drive a fast car ☐

Enjoy a multiplicity of sexual partners ☐

Explore your erogenous zones ☐

Banish those wrinkles ☐

Shed half your body weight ☐

Give birth in a birthing pool ☐
Bungee jump in the Grand Canyon ☐
Swim with dolphins ☐
Swim with sharks ☐
Discover the power of Now ☐
Visit every continent ☐
Visit every country ☐
Think big ☐
Get ripped ☐
Sunbathe on a playboy's yacht ☐
Join the Mile High Club ☐
Struggle to contain your curves ☐
Come back stronger from heartbreak ☐
Publish a bestseller ☐
See the following animals in the wild:
    Amur tiger ☐
    Snow leopard ☐
    Honduran ghost bat ☐
    Komodo dragon ☐
Own an infinity pool ☐
Sign a prenuptial agreement ☐
Earn a black credit card ☐
Remember a past life ☐
Make headlines ☐
Play with your inner child ☐

- [ ] Eat exclusively protein
- [ ] Work out in a hypoxic chamber
- [ ] Uncover the secrets of an A-list body
- [ ] Check yourself into rehab
- [ ] Receive an honorary degree
- [ ] Harness your subconscious mind
- [ ] Downsize to a condo
- [ ] Tip a doorman twice his monthly wage
- [ ] Raise awareness for a fee
- [ ] Buy a vineyard
- [ ] Make love on a tiger skin rug
- [ ] Build a basement under your basement
- [ ] Pull yourself up by the bootstraps
- [ ] Pay heed to a water sommelier
- [ ] Get blooded
- [ ] Learn to fly your private jet
- [ ] Master the universal Law of Attraction
- [ ] Launch a new fragrance
- [ ] Adopt a beautiful brown baby
- [ ] Sell exclusive rights to *Hello!*
- [ ] Have them augmented
- [ ] Use the panic room
- [ ] Visit your vault
- [ ] Experience Zero-g weightlessness
- [ ] Help to save Africa

- View the Earth from space ☐
- Feel humbled by your success ☐
- Make your child a movie star ☐
- Endanger you septum ☐
- Compliment your private chef ☐
- Punch your anger management coach ☐
- Read the books in your library ☐
- Establish a think tank ☐
- Prove litigious ☐
- Look at the art you own ☐
- Trade up for a younger model ☐
- Know Jesus loves you ☐
- Experience opulent solitude ☐
- Taste gold ☐
- Make the cover of *Forbes* ☐
- Sue for defamation ☐
- Find a complaisant guru ☐
- Have sex with a lookalike ☐
- Endow your alma mater ☐
- Invest in tar sands ☐
- Own a football club ☐
- Intervene editorially ☐
- Fail to visit every room in your house ☐
- Silence a critic ☐
- Find a warm welcome on your island ☐

Deny a conflict of interests ☐
Shoot an elephant between the eyes ☐
Purchase a live organ ☐
Achieve a monopoly ☐
Pay for your own facts ☐
Quash disruptive technology ☐
Disinherit your children ☐
Hire a food taster ☐
Watch a pool boy make love to your wife ☐
Alter government policy ☐
Issue explicit instructions not to be looked at ☐
Keep tigers in your garden ☐
Finance a coup ☐
Establish plausible denial ☐
Bury the facts ☐
Bury the fact-finders ☐
Establish a religious cult ☐
Install a missile-defence system ☐
Build a hypoallergenic bomb shelter ☐
Invest all your hopes in cloning ☐
Consider cryogenic burial ☐
Keep your hands clean ☐
Try forbidden flesh ☐
Work out what was in it for you ☐
Think you got away with it ☐

What gets lost

Bunking off

The first thing Graham did upon waking was to check his teeth. He pressed them gingerly with his thumb before giving the incisors a tug. They seemed firm. In his dream, a recurring one, they had come loose, crumbling from his mouth.

His wife slept on. The alarm clock stared. NO POINT NOT GETTING UP, it said.

Looking in the fridge, Graham found the marmalade gunged up and cold. She had left it in overnight. He couldn't hope to spread it now. He settled for plain toast but the margarine she'd bought was too salty and he scraped the excess into the bin.

His wife moaned. With Billy gone there was no point getting up. She paid no attention to the grapefruit juice he brought her with its swirling cloud of pulp. Graham made deliberate noise with the foil. He arranged the pills as usual beside her glass.

On the train there was the usual overcrowding. Many fragrances, pleasant on their own, blended into a miasma. Graham turned his face towards the Perspex screen. He imagined he had a pocket of air just for him and breathed it as though secretly. The screen was smudged with grease from people's bodies.

Clouds all the colours of a bruise churned above the City. A storm coming, Graham hoped, but he had forgotten about it by the time he was sitting at his desk, the first coffee of the day giving up its puny ghost beside him. The desk had been swept clean of personal effects. It could have been anybody's.

All morning familiar heads swayed behind the partition. Graham went out for lunch; it had rained in the world. He wiped with his sleeve the fat drops from his habitual bench in Bunhill Fields and ate a sandwich, wondering all the time how in God's name he was supposed to break it to her.

Later, in the glib sheen of the toilet mirror, he checked his gums where he'd felt the pressure. He could see nothing more unpleasant than usual.

Graham worked until five. "Bunking off," he said to the post room girl, the sight of whose padded breasts he thought he might miss.

Nick Burke caught up with him in the atrium. He pretended to have been running. Calling it "voluntary", Graham reflected as they shook hands, only made it easier for those who were staying.

His wife had gone to her sister's. She had put the marmalade back in the fridge. Graham decided not to mind, remembering the dream about his teeth.

Cryptozoology

People in town had got the measure of him. They knew his sort: the wild-eyed fanatic, the desert guru, driven by God knows what distress to the crucible of flies. What was he searching for? Some ruddy goanna: extinct, dead as a rock; but not for him.

The man was no scientist but he declared that an advantage. He had, he said, seen enough of them to know the smallness of their minds, the meanness of their superior smiles. For a month he had been going on his expeditions: heading out in his Japanese car into the Wilcolo Valley, or patrolling Wilpena Creek among the red gums and native pines.

Nobody knew much about him. He was polite and he paid: there's saner men you can't say the same about. Once he left his wallet in the pub. Before handing it back, Phil Tucker checked inside. There was a photo of a little girl, maybe three, standing in striped socks and a cutesy white dress on a paving slab. There was another photo, more recent by the look of it, of a teenage brunette – good-looking – all dressed up for a ball.

There was something about the owner put Phil Tucker off asking questions.

In March, when the heat lessened, the city came up to the Ranges. It mistook the man for local colour. The bush had dried him up, like an apple core. His eyes were raw with looking. He turned them on the student who challenged him in the pub.

"I've seen them as fossils," the young man said. "I think you'll find they died out in the Ice Age."

The man had known this before: people tramping all over his theories. There's always a chance, he said. A herpetologist had startled one in the Wattagan Mountains. A French priest had seen one in Papua New Guinea.

Witnesses are fallible, the student replied. The ape turns out to be a hoax, the lizard is a log, the sea serpent is the erect penis of a Grey whale. Why not focus on the marvels that *live* and which by our actions we are losing?

Nobody had seen the goanna man angry before. The blood

drained from his face. He gripped the counter, his knuckles bleached with rage. What about the coelacanth, he said, dredged up alive from prehistory? What about the ivory-billed woodpecker, or the Wollemi Pine, shade once to dinosaurs, secretly ramifying in the Blue Mountains? Sometimes the world gives second chances.

The whole pub had gone quiet. The challenger backed off, showing his palms. He knew better than to puncture the illusion: that it's possible, if you search hard enough, to find something living that is thought lost forever.

Sepiatone

At the age of seventy-eight, my grandfather became invisible. One moment he was seated in his easy chair, sullen as ever, a drop of fluid balanced on the tip of his nose; the next, his skin grew transparent, his hair thinned to gossamer. Grandma threw her knitting pattern into the air and screamed. She begged him to come back but Grandpa looked at her blankly, and his eyes too became transparent, so that I could see through them to the antimacassar.

Grandma gripped me by the sleeve. "Do something," she cried. My grandfather was in no pain; indeed, he seemed unaware of his predicament until he looked at his hands and saw blood, clear as water, pumping through the veins.

At that moment, something astonishing happened. Grandpa smiled. It wasn't a particularly kindly smile, more embarrassed really, but it was quite definitely a smile. In all my childhood, throughout my unspeakable adolescence, never had such a thing occurred. I could just make out the white of his teeth in the mist of his face; the two gold molars had turned a sepia colour.

"Don't just sit there," said Grandma. "Fetch someone or we'll lose him for ever."

But it was already too late. My grandfather had become no more substantial than steam in a breeze. By the time Grandma's hands left her horrified face, there remained nothing of him, not even a faint outline. I put out my hand and reached for the space that I supposed my grandfather to occupy. It was empty.

Over the next few days, to be a comfort, I fell back on old clichés. Just because we couldn't see him didn't mean he wasn't there; invisibility was a disability like any other; medical science was advancing in leaps and bounds. Above all, it was vital for us to continue as normal. We didn't want to alienate Grandpa in his time of need. So we made food for him, which we placed at the table next to our own. When enough of these dishes had gone untouched, I tried to convince Grandma that his behaviour was quite normal, all part of the adjustment process. When Grandpa stopped raiding the fridge, however, we changed tactics.

It was clear that he had taken to his potting shed: I could see the kerosene lamp burning at night. So his meals waited outside while we chewed ours indoors, and at nightfall I would return half empty plates from the garden. Faintly encouraged, Grandma took to preparing elaborate dishes to tempt him back, finding new purpose in her culinary mission. Day after day I was sent out to buy chillies and peppers, saffron and ginger, rice wine and naan bread. When these failed to get results, Grandma changed strategy and, for the first time in fifty years of marriage, she treated him to ketchup and chips, cod in batter, sausage and beans. For a while this new tactic paid off and, in return, my grandfather etched complex patterns into the grease with his cutlery, which my Grandma studied avidly, holding the plates up to the light. It seemed like the situation might last, but in her mounting hopefulness my grandmother made a mistake. She took to slipping notes beneath the plates, perfume-dabbed love letters like the ones she hid in the box beneath the stairs.

My grandfather's final disappearance happened more slowly than the first (though, looking back on it now, I should have foreseen that too) and it began with the returning of his dishes untouched. Night after night, I walked back to the house with the loaded tray, my heart heavy, trying to persuade myself that he was only out of sorts, not himself for the moment.

"Not himself?" Grandma said. "What *is* he now? You tell me!"

Tired of waiting, we broke into the potting shed. The smell was terrible, like burnt molasses. Empty crisp packets and chocolate wrappers lay strewn about the floor. And there, pinned to the wall with a Stanley-knife, were my grandmother's late letters of love. I watched as Grandma took the knife and picked up the stained pieces of paper. She looked at them blankly for a moment. Her head jerked as though she were about to retch, and she cast the letters to the ground. "The bugger. The bloody – buggering – *bugger*. Oh, he was always a cold one. He never cared for us, never. I'll bet he's waited for this to happen all his life."

She hid her face in her hands and sobbed. Her crying sounded to me unpleasantly girlish. I bent down and picked up one of the love letters. Despite the sickly sweetness in the air, I could just make out the smell of perfume from the paper. I held the letter to the light. Her signature had been carefully scored out with a blade.

One finger exercise

On the last day of his despair, Alasdair remembered his father's pistol, stored ever since the end of the war in the cherry wood cabinet across the hall. He located the tiny key that would unlock it behind a wall of sheet music in one of the leather-bound ashtrays his father used to collect.

Alasdair held the key teeth-side up under the trap of his fingers. It was nine months to the day since his diagnosis. "Nothing fatal," the doctor had assured him. Dupuytren's Contracture: it sounded like an exercise for spanning the keys.

Refusing at first to believe it, he had gone home to resume his assimilation of Bach's *Partitas and Fugues*. But having a name for his condition made it worsen rapidly. Trying to find a simple chord, his fingers flinched and curled up like wounded animals. The contracture was vicelike; the more he exercised, the harder it bit, until his hands were agonised paddles floundering on the keys. Occasionally he would have days of remission but they were grace notes in his life and soon ceased altogether.

His hands had warped, his life also, for he had driven away his friends and sympathetic colleagues. The Bach sheet music was locked away in the piano stool; he spent entire days in the sunlight of a disregarded summer, watching his fingers furl up like scorched leaves.

On the day, early in the Festival, when he had been scheduled to play the *Partitas and Fugues*, Alasdair had received a visit from the Musicians' Benevolent Fund which had put him in a rage and made him weep as soon as the woman was gone.

Thus he came to stand beside the cabinet.

When he was little, his father used to show him the pistol. It was always loaded, he said, in case of burglars. *Or for naughty boys who don't practise their scales.* Alasdair had no idea if the pistol still worked. While the father had fought in a war and killed men, his son had little experience outside music.

It was a cool afternoon of scudding cloud when he entered the gardens. Jugglers were spinning sticks on the grass. A group of students was handing out fliers. He passed them all on his way up the hill. His father used to bring him here, under the dark volcanic crags, to speak of God and music, of the purpose he was born for. His father had not approved of the festival. He frowned on dramatics and all pretending.

Alasdair found a suitable spot, extracted the heavy object from his pocket and lifted its cold snout to his temple.

For perhaps no more than a fraction of a second, he would have been able to smell unseen flowers.

The group of students found him unconscious but uninjured, a replica pistol in his clenched and ruined fist. Somebody wondered if he wasn't famous.

The runner

Night bombardment, and the telephone wires cut to shreds, the observation officer had an urgent message to send down the line. Reclus was summoned from his vigil on the fire-step.

The officer was hoarse from shouting. Men said he had an uncle in the top brass. "See that he gets it in person," he said to Reclus. "I want you to put it in his hand."

There were no pilots to chart him through the wasteland, and little light save for the field-battery that revealed in flashes stripped trees, an eviscerated horse, stretches of churned mud powdered with chloride of lime. Reclus could not run for the rottenness of the boards. The going was cold slime, then hard and firm again underfoot. He ducked where he remembered the slack wires. The annunciation of each incoming shell made him stoop and grimace.

In a bombed-out part of the trench, the water was more like slobber than anything. Men were dredging the broken section, turning up unspeakable things. Reclus gulped air through his mouth and waded into the ditch.

A solitary star-shell rose from the Bosches. Reclus' long shadow contracted as the shell reached its apex, then lengthened again, so that he saw a jerking puppet. Something exploded metres short and he stumbled against the hastily thrown-up earth. Loose dirt tumbled from the split hessian of sandbags and spilled cold on his nape. High-pitched screaming broke the caul of his deafness. Stretcher-bearers passed, smelling of iodine and cordite and piss.

He moved faster as he left the hottest trenches. Artillerymen, evenly spaced, sent their nightlines twinkling in the damp and stunted blackness. Reclus knew the places in this sector that were enfiladed: his lover had collapsed in blood and shit a week ago at one of them. His tongue was foul in his mouth as he leapt through these unhealthy points. He held his breath as if that might save him from a sniper's bullet.

In the first glimmer of dawn, Reclus bolted down a transport line towards the transport wagons and the field kitchens. The walking wounded moaned and huddled. Reclus gave one water, another a damp cigarette. He scurried close to the wagon lines, in memory perhaps of his childhood and the hot breath of horses. Others, without urgent errands, moved like elderly workmen and cast the broken nets of their gaze upon him.

It was strange, as ever, penetrating the grounds of the chateau. Reclus felt like a visitor from another planet. Waved through by sentries, he made his way to the great hall where the general sat nursing his morning bowl of coffee.

Reclus stepped up to the desk with its maps and ashtrays and handsome chessboard. He shivered with cold after the heat of his run and there was a log fire burning but he was not invited to approach it. Standing to attention, he tried to stretch out the ache in his back.

The general received the sweat-stained paper. Responsibility so weighed on his brow that he barely raised his eyes. He read the message, frowned and dismissed its bearer. Closing the door on his way out, Reclus saw the general read the message again, sigh, and move his opponent's queen to take his bishop.

Time & the janitor

In about twenty seconds you're going to throw up. Please do it into that funnel.

There – feeling better? Take a glucose tablet. Time plays havoc with the old blood sugar.

I shouldn't bother – that's twenty inches of fibre-reinforced plastic. We don't know where you're from. We don't know what you're carrying. Believe me, it's as much in your interest as it is in ours.

What were you expecting – dignitaries? Those days are long gone. You're the trickle after the flood. You're the drop of piss in the underpants of time.

Sorry. I forget my manners. It's just we've had all sorts pass through the portal. Maniacs, most of them. Crooks and gamblers.

I say "we" but in fact I'm pretty much the last one here. I used to have a life outside. I used to see the world. Now I wait for the future to turn up – or those bits that get through before they cancel each other out.

Good idea, take the weight off. That's what the chair's for. You might as well make your stay a comfortable one.

I'm afraid there is no one else you can talk to. I'm as high as these things go. I have authorisation.

What did I say – all sorts pass through? You don't imagine you're the first, do you? I mean, it's not like there's a chronological order. And where else are you lot going to turn up, if not here? Time travel being like the telephone, you need two machines – one now and another in the future – for any communication to take place. The boffins – and I'm not one of them, so don't expect me to get technical – they reckoned the portal would change our world. Turns out it changed yours. As soon as it was built, a flood of you arrived from the future. Not to save humanity, mind. Not to teach us about peace and love and how to build a fusion reactor. Oh no. The greatest scientific triumph in human history and all to place a bet on the Grand National.

I'll grant you, motivations this end were not much better. The gift of hindsight? Only if there was money to be made from it. We cut deals with the canny ones who guessed what would appeal to our masters.

Stole a technological march on our competitors. We got a head start on the future and you got to tweak the past to your advantage. Only we hadn't thought things through. Because each new arrival was coming from a *different possible* future. Each future shut down other futures – euthanised this genius, set that criminal mastermind on a path to dentistry. The flood of visitors became a trickle. Each new arrival was cancelling out his or her successors. Sometimes even his own ancestors. Now *those* were the really spectacular visits. I don't suppose you've ever seen a space-time paradox implosion? Anyway, the upshot of it all is quarantine. We can't let you out. Can't let you tamper with history. Which, don't forget, is destiny for us.

Go back, you say? Step back through there? Oh dear, oh dear. Didn't you know? The telephone analogy isn't watertight. This portal's receiver only.

Now there's no sense in wearing yourself out. Please sit down. Sit down or we'll have to pacify you.

There. Catch your breath.

I hope you don't think this is personal. There are rules. There are protocols. If you're still here tomorrow my superiors will want to debrief you. It's a simple enough procedure. It won't hurt. What happens then? Let's not trouble ourselves trying to second-guess the future.

Human rights? I don't think they come into it. After all, you've not yet been conceived.

Sound proofed. What's that? No one can hear you. Except me, and I'm only the janitor. That's the thing about scientific miracles. There's always some poor bugger who has to stay behind to tidy up the mess.

The Dirty Realist Choose Your Own Adventure Book

Try as you might, you cannot unscrew the cap. It's locked tight, like some witch has placed a goddamn curse upon it. If you decide to use your teeth, turn to page 32. If you smash the bottle and drink from the broken neck, turn to page 56.

She lies down, complaining of the heat. You don't say anything, even though she's about to roll her ass over the soiled patch. You sit quietly on the edge of the mattress and watch as she writhes, making small cat noises. Is it worth the effort? If yes, turn to page 104. If no, turn to page 9.

Even after twenty days, you still can't believe this girl is your daughter. She stands in your garage, so lank and ungainly that you find yourself resenting her. She asks if she can do anything to help. Does she know about cars? Would she recognise a wrench from a spanner? If yes, turn to page 28. If no, turn to page 80.

Long after she's gone, you're still picking hairs out of your teeth. Not even the taste of mouthwash can chase the numbness away. Do you go to your son's baseball game like you promised (page 24), or do you find that bottle you stowed under the pickup (page 71)?

She hands you the monkey wrench and you stare at her, impressed. You let her stay on while you slide under the truck. Lying there, you can't help admiring her legs. If you feel ashamed, turn to page 42. If you keep looking despite your best efforts, turn to page 117.

The baseball game is sparsely attended. Some goofball is wearing a corncob outfit. You look for your son in the field but can't make him out. Surely you haven't got the date wrong? You check your wristwatch but remember it's broken. If you ask the fat dad next to you, turn to page 27. If you decide to stick it out despite your thirst, turn to page 51.

Even though she offers, you turn her down. She doesn't seem at all disappointed – in fact she looks relieved – but all the same you worry she'll feel rejected. Do you tell her lies about your potency? Go to page 70. Do you force yourself to give her a kiss? Go to page 64.

Your neighbour, Peggy, stands grinning behind the fly screen. You take a deep breath, guessing what she's come for. If you invite her inside, turn to page 13. If you decide to make an excuse, turn to page 43.

She tells you she made it all up. She isn't kin. Once you spoke kindly to her Mom is all. Ever since, she has loved you from a distance. She begins to weep. Do you kick her out? Go to page 90. If you feel sorry for her and decide to let her stay, go to page 12.

You spend the day in bed. Turn back to page 1.

What gets lost

Finally made it to the village. Our guide got hopelessly lost – like a drunk who can't find his way around his own backyard. After wading through bogs and practically breathing mosquitoes, we were welcomed by the elders. They seem shocked to learn that we lost our path.

It is not a good sign. In the past the spirits guided us, so long as we spoke their names and places.

Yuri asked who was most likely to remember the old folk remedies. Our best bet is an elderly woman who lives near the river. She received us without a hint of suspicion.

He wants to ask me about the forest plants? What can I tell him? I have forgotten so many of their names.

Bad diarrhea. Confined to our hut but Yuri has been making friends with Galina. I guess she feels more at ease with her one of her own countrymen.

I find I must take such wandering journeys through your language to say what would have taken a moment in my own. I am not used to talking like this. I have spoken more in three days than I did in a month. But these words are like dry grass in my throat.

The old woman is small, moon-faced. She doesn't smell too good but why should she? Everyone here stinks.

What can I tell you about the forest? What can I say about the plants that heal? I have forgotten the word for the whispering of birch leaves in a storm, for the flapping of an eagle's wings. I have forgotten the words that used to describe every feature of a hill, so that no one could lose their way upon it.

Her mind is defective so we play things by the book. Try to jog her memory: dig up old stories, creation myths.

It had something to do with a duck. There was an egg at the beginning of the world. Tell your American I cannot remember. Nobody here can. I am the last speaker of our language. My children can understand it but they will not speak it. My grandchildren barely recognise a word.

Lots of reminiscences, scant progress. Was this trip a mistake? Siberia's a barren place for ethnobotanical research. And I'm sick to death of reindeer meat.

Do you see that jacket, that hat? They belonged to our last storyteller. He was a shaman – in my parents' day. Sometimes his stories would go on for many nights. He was taken away in the great white month.

Another frustrating day. The old lady is cagey. What has Yuri been telling her?

I was only a girl but he had no one else who wanted to learn from him. Before he died he agreed to teach me. I learned many of the stories but it is years since I told them. Who would listen now? Who would understand?

Galina refuses to speak to us – or to anybody. She's been locked in her cabin for days. Yuri says she's remembering. Remembering what? He shrugs, inscrutable.

If birds live in the sky and fish in the water, old people live in silence. I will die next year. I can feel the bones sharp against my skin. But I am no longer afraid. It has taken great effort and pain but I have come out of the chrysalis. The stories are at my back like wings. I shall fly with them one last time.

Yuri did not even alert me to what was going on. He's become so quiet and uncooperative. I went looking for him and found him standing in a clearing, looking towards the bank of the river. He gestured to me to be quiet and I saw what he was watching. The old girl has gone crazy.

She was wearing that tatty waistcoat and hat – the ones from the nail on her wall. She was sitting on her own by the river, on a tree stump. In her lap was a bowl of something – tea? And she was shaking drops of it into the river and the grass from a kind of strainer. I swear she was talking to the air. It was like a performance, not a song exactly but an incantation, a prayer that went on and on, until the sun set. I guess she was telling her stories, the ones I wanted to hear, that might contain some useful information. Her words came in gusts towards us but Yuri could not understand them. Let the wind carry them, he said, weirding me out. Wherever it will take them.

Bookends

Bibliophagy

In the noble history of our Resistance, one death stands out for its strange defiance. That it was an act of defiance did not immediately occur to the enemy. The harassed coroner delivered a verdict of suicide brought on by insanity. It suited our foes to believe as much – or as little – but we know better and commend the sacrifice of Mr H.

From the information available it would appear that Mr H, a bachelor, inherited his library from his father and grandfather, both of them notable patriots. His one eccentricity involved his beloved cats, which he would send after their deaths to a local bookbinder. The policeman who discovered Mr H's remains might have noticed on his depleted bookshelves all six volumes of Gibbon bound in tabby and calico fur.

Mr H's corpse was surrounded by shreds of paper, half-digested boluses of vellum and empty bindings discarded like oyster shells. It is evident that, at the darkest time for our nation, Mr H locked himself away and set to eating all those books which would, he correctly surmised, be proscribed by our enemy. His death must have been an agonising one; yet he persisted, carefully detaching page by page from its binding with a decorative paper knife. Sometimes, with leather covers, he appears to have boiled them down and swallowed strips with brandy. His water-meter suggests a great consumption of water. The project must have taken several weeks.

The Resistance heralds the significance of this act of protest. For comparison one must look to Jan Palach or the Buddhist monk, Thích Quảng Đức. Unlike these protestors, however, Mr H went on to defy his enemies *after* death. In his will (which has subsequently disappeared from the Records Office), Mr H left money for a certain provision: that he be flayed by his friend the bookbinder and his skin used as the binding for a photograph album. The authorities, not yet recognising the significance of this request, gave up the body. One of our agents has seen the result. The photographs in the album depict Mr H's family over the course of a century. On the last page a black and white photograph shows a boy, presumed to be Mr H, seated in a dappled arbour with a great volume of poetry open on his knees.

All who knew Mr H considered him a gentleman: a primary school teacher of thirty years and a keen amateur writer who retired early to pursue his literary ambitions. Who would have suspected him capable of martyrdom? Evidently it was the intolerable affront of occupation that spurred him to it. Confronted by tyranny he consumed his books and saved them from the bonfire. After his death Mr H (who never found a publisher), sealed his defiance by becoming a book himself. Thus we can conclude of him as John Earle in his *Microcosmographie* did of the antiquarian: "His grave does not fright him for he has been used to sepulchres, and he likes death the better because it gathers him to his fathers."

Essential words of the Empress Shōtoku

Feeling her death upon her – that last and implacable courtier – the empress Shōtoku vacated the throne and took to her bed. Neither elaborate ritual nor the studied expressions of mildness on the faces of her servants could conceal a general fear of contagion; for the boils were stark and angry, white-tipped craters, in the ravaged imperial face, and a smell came off her that all the perfumes of Asia could not mask.

In the world that would continue without her, the cold weather was closing in. Decay swept past her open window: leaves shredded from cherry boughs, birds like strips of cloth tossed hither and thither by the autumn wind.

From all over the empire, officers of many ranks were gathering for the ritual of the Eight Readings.

The Empress moaned. It was difficult, through the fog of her pain, to discern the lineaments of her achievement. Still, the physicians held off with their salves and potions, for she wanted to keep her mind clear before the end.

In the night, she cried out for her friend, the Lady Himegimi, who was summoned from her apartments. "What troubles your Majesty," Himegimi asked, glad for once of the formality that prevented her from touching the Empress.

Shōtoku muttered of fire and ashes.

The Lady Himegimi assured the Empress that her legacy was secure, that in her wisdom she had defeated all rebellion and ensured stability for years to come. The Empress toiled to breathe; she fought not to claw at her face. At last she slept, and the ghosts who visited her could not agree on her name. To her father, who smiled at her while filling his quiver with arrows, she was the princess Abe-hime. To the poet and courtier Nakamaro, she was Kōken, the pliable and credulous young empress. She looked Nakamaro again, bowing before the executioner's sword, and the name that flew from his lips across the waters of Lake Biwa was Shōtoku, tyrant and whore of the monk Dōkyō.

The Empress awoke with a fever. For a time she did not know

who she was, for her essential name eluded her. Perhaps she *had* no essence beneath the layers of silk and custom, nothing solid and unchanging by which to know herself. A frosty day dawned and her fever abated. She remembered how, as Kōken, she had become a tool for Nakamaro. That misfortune, and the forced abdication that followed, had taught her the power of names to efface dishonour. Under her final name, that still clung to her as she clung to life, she had reclaimed the Chrysanthemum Throne and destroyed her many enemies.

A bowl of soup was brought to her but she could not eat it; nor could she recall, in daylight, whether she had dreamt the visit of the Lady Himegimi. In the afternoon, a clearing opened briefly in the thorny wood of her delirium and she glimpsed the form of her legacy. The vision eased a little of her pain. Summoning the abbot, she told him to bring her one of the stupas, a miniature wooden pagoda, from the palace temple, so that she might hear again the *dharani-sutra*, those essential words printed on her orders on the longest strips of paper ever made.

The abbot performed as he was tasked; and so, with monks to chant the words that would outlast the ruin of her age, the Empress listened to the distillation of human knowledge. One million stupas had been constructed and dispatched throughout the empire. Each contained, in prayer form, a key to the universe, ascending in circles from earth to the heavens and wound about the Buddha's staff.

"Again," the Empress whispered, and the words were chanted, over and over, into the Month of Frost, into the mouth of darkness, monks taking turns, with eyes averted from the imperial bed, to build temples of prayer with their voices, until the monk Dōkyō, who owed his temporal power to her favour, lifted a lantern to his mistress's face and saw that she had taken leave of the world and all the names to which she had answered while she lived.

A pillow book

"*Delivered.* I resent the use of that word."

"Why, for heaven's sake?"

"You make it sound like a baby."

"Well consider. There's the pleasure of conception, then the slog of gestation. Those pains in your lumbar, the bursts of impatience. You even find yourself prey to strange appetites."

"That slut in publicity, for instance."

"What an imagination you have, darling. You should consider writing fiction. But no more interruptions please; a sustained metaphor is going begging. You object to my use of the word 'delivery', as though somehow something that everyone does – from the milkman to the centre forward – belongs only to women in parturition."

"You always use long words when I'm on a short fuse."

"It seems quite the right word to me. I have conceived and I have laboured…"

"Oh Jesus."

"What?"

"This is typical of you: *typical*. The one thing women have over men and men rub their grubby metaphors all over it. Delivered indeed. You needed more help for this 'delivery' than any hospital could provide. No peremptory epidural for you, no rushed visits from the overloaded midwife. For you it was smooth sailing and you haven't a scar to show for it, with your readers and advisers, your givers of tea and sympathy, your indulgent wife, your cosseting agent, your assiduous secretary, and even – dear God, in *this* day and age! – even a bloody typist."

"You ought to approve: I'm keeping the sisterhood in curry."

"Sometimes I can't believe your cheek."

"Yours are growing blotchy, dear."

"You insufferable conceited *middle-aged*… You cannot possibly have the faintest notion what you're talking about. Look! *This.* Through an aperture like *that.* Can you have any conception of the agony involved?"

"I assure you, my darling, that's not how melons come into the world. Helena… Sweet one…. Let's not quarrel. Today was a happy day. You should be glad for me."

"Bully for you. Back to the fun of the book fair."

"You know I don't enjoy them."

"Oh I'm sure it's a great burden: all that attention, those trustafarian groupies…"

"Now you're being ridiculous."

"You have form."

"What?"

"You have *form*."

"My God, you have a sweet tooth for poison memories."

"Don't mix your metaphors."

"It was six years ago. Six *years*. I've forgotten about it, why can't you? You're like a dog with its bone."

"And you're a conceited ape. *Women in parturition*. You should listen to yourself. You're so pompous. And so *wrong*. What the hell would you know about childbearing? The largest thing you'll ever have to pass is a kidney stone."

"Imaginative sympathy, my darling. It is my profession. And more to the point, now that we've strayed into dreary literalism… much more to our purpose, ever since you decided to leap all tongues blazing on my innocent use of an everyday word… let me ask you, my beloved companion, after all our years together, what the hell would *you* know about bearing children?"

The bard's last words

What was he doing, the old man, so far from his hearth and kinsmen? Flinching from the wind's talons, ploughing a field of snow, he thought of Eadwin who should inherit his verses. The boy was covetous of his word-hoard but the old man had given him nothing, only harsh phrases and scolding looks. A greying head in the wilderness, he was not a warrior, no feeder of ravens, but a teller of tales with a question on his back.

He had borne it since the wedding feast when, under the banner of the golden dragon, he had plucked his harp and conjured the hot breath of battle. The poem had taken him three seasons to compose: hard nights weaving on the loom of memory. In the mead hall the warriors heard again the spear-din and their scars ached with remembrance. When it was finished and his harp had quivered to stillness, they bellowed and belched: yes, it was even thus, a glorious victory, their greatest since they wrested from the Britons their Paradise of Powys.

In Eadwin the old man saw the triumph that ought to have been his. Outside of battle, to add to the songs of Mercia was most glorious. Yet he did not feel exalted. One pair of eyes, among all the brow-stars shining in the hall, had looked at him dully. Even as he tasted glory, one face turned away and, turning, made the poet's heart a stone. He was in pursuit of that dissenting head.

Yet now the fangs of winter closed about his chest. He feared that he would leave his bones on the hillside, to be bleached of questions by the sun and rain. Only the tinkling of a sheep's bell roused him from a final slumber. Strong hands wrenched him from the glaze ice. There were smells of dung and wood smoke. He lay beside a fire in the black womb of a hut.

"It's you," he said. "You turned away from my recitation."
"The tale was told."
"Our eye-paths crossed and you left the hall."
"I've no one left to guard my sheep."

The shepherd was not of the lord's hall. Rank and ceremony were as legends to him, who understood the fire that is locked in gorse, the juice that rises in new heather. He was a churl, unworthy of remembrance in a *scop*'s verses, yet permitted at the wedding feast.

The old man asked him about his song.

When the shepherd had spoken, he gave the visitor broth and left him to sleep beside the embers of the fire.

In the morning the snow began to melt and the teller of tales walked home. His pupil looked for him on the battlements and ran through the ice meal to greet him.

Eadwin asked many questions and, with eager eyes, hounded the old man for answers. But his master would not speak of his encounter on the hillside. He retired to his bed and slept for a day and a night.

When the poet awoke, his pupil greeted him with bread and broth. The old man regained some strength and soon he was pestered for his battle song. "Let me hear it," the boy said. "Let me keep it alive for hearers yet unborn." But the old man would teach him only the former songs of Mercia: those he had inherited from his forebears. After many weeks, Eadwin's eyes filled with tears, yet still the poet would not unlock his word-hoard.

Age caught up with him. Heavily he lifted his bones and the world contracted to the dark womb of his hut. When the next feast came, his lord became angry, for he was denied a performance of the battle song. The *scop* pleaded infirmity and waited, with munching gums, as if for an unknown guest.

A monk was sent from Worcester to trap the poet's song in a cage of vellum. Eadwin received him with hollow eyes. Twice the monk was admitted to the poet's bedside; twice he left with a weary refusal.

Neither pupil nor scribe would ever understand. The battle with the Welsh, which had united Mercia and Wessex and furnished the old man with his subject, had robbed the shepherd of his three sons. All but one in the world had praised the poet's song. Yet the poet knew his song's worth and he let it die within him.

The translation of Archie Gloag

These fragments are the poet's last words, written in August 2005.
In August 2005, the famous Scottish poet wrote these final fragments.
Here are the master's ultimate fragments, composed in August 2005.

– Between the bewilderment of pain and the morphine fog, a few moments of clarity. As if a window were opened in the closed room of my dying.

Between the bafflement of pain and the fog of morphine, I experience a few moments of clarity. As if one had opened a window in the shut bedroom where I am dying.

For a few moments, between the wilderness of pain and the mist of morphine, I know clearness. As if a window had been thrown open in my death-chamber.

– This taking leave of life is hard work. I dream that I am sitting my Finals again, though I have not prepared and the questions hide from me like silverfish under the stapled fold. I know I shall pass this final examination. I fear to do so and fear the labour of it. The fear and the labour, and the drugs they use to ease both, occupy me entirely. Dying is a consuming present. Only briefly can the commonplace questions be entertained.

It is hard work, this departing from life. I have a dream that I am taking my final university examinations, although I have not revised for them and the questions seem to hide from me, like silverfish, under the folded and stapled paper. I know I shall pass this final examination. I am afraid, both of doing so and of the work that doing so will involve. This fear, and the drugs they use to allay it, entirely occupies me. One dies consumed by the present moment. Only briefly can one ask oneself the ordinary questions.

What hard work this dying is. I have dreams that I am sitting my final examination, for which I have not revised. Under the creases and staples of the paper, silvery fish conceal themselves

like questions. I know I will pass this last examination. I am afraid of doing so and of the effort of it. The fear and the effort, and the drugs they use to put me at ease, occupy me completely. Dying is a gift that consumes us. It is possible to amuse oneself with everyday questions only for brief moments.

– Has it been worth it? Do those slim volumes on the shelf I can no longer see speak in defence of the life I was given? Were they worth the pain I inflicted, the self-importance that cut me off from my fellow beings?

Has it been worth the trouble? Do those slender books on the shelf – a shelf I can no longer see – plead for me at the tribunal of life? Do they justify the pain I caused, the sense of grandeur that divorced me from my fellow beings?

Has it been worth it? Do those thin volumes on the now invisible shelf speak up to defend the life that was given to me? Are they worth the pain I inflicted, my ego that cut me off from other people?

– I devoted myself to writing and translating. In the latter I experienced perhaps my most intense engagement with other minds. But what, truly, did I connect with? Was I chasing a chimera: the hope that essence can be carried across from one language to another? *Traduttore traditore.* How fitting that I, too, shall soon be *trans latus* – translated into another idiom: perhaps the silence of that chasm into which we cast our poems, never knowing where they might land.

I have dedicated myself to literature and translation. I have experienced, in the latter, perhaps my most ardent connection with other minds. Yet in truth, with what did I connect? Was it a mythical beast that I pursued: the hope that essence can be transported from one language to another? Traduttore traditore. How just it seems that, soon, I too shall be trans latus *– translated into another idiom: the silence, perhaps, of that chasm into which we cast our verses, never knowing where they might land.*

I have devoted my life to writing and translating. Perhaps I was never more intensely affianced to other minds than in the second

of these. But what, in truth, did I connect with? Was I chasing a chimera *[a monster in Greek myth – tr.]* in the hope that what is essential can be carried over from one language into another? *Traduttore traditore [Italian: "translator, traitor" -tr.].* How appropriate that I too shall soon be trans latus *[Latin: "brought across"- tr.]* into another dialect, like the silence in that trench where we moulded our poems, never knowing where they might end up.

Flow

It was, Elaine Crowder considered on her flight south, a good thing there were no living relatives to complicate matters. The Savoyards would be obliging: she was, after all, the foremost authority; they could rely on her to manage the world's attention. Scanning the press release on her laptop, it occurred to her that this final act in the Life would put her, its author, centre stage. She had become her subject's contemporary.

The plane landed in Turin where the heat was oppressive, and she was glad of the taxi's air conditioning as it sped her, through Alpine splendour, to Chamonix and the goal of her pilgrimage.

Time was of the essence. For eighty years it had, in the bonds of glacial ice, preserved the body of Alice Purdue, but now the poet was returned to the laws of decay, and her most devoted acolyte had only a few hours to observe the corpse *in situ* before the authorities transferred it to the cold of a mortuary cabinet.

Elaine was greeted by Yvan, the mountaineer who had made the discovery. She was sure he noticed the way her clothes clung to her in the heat, the sweat that beaded her forehead.

Yvan drove them to the village of Argentiere. On the way he talked about the retreat of the glaciers. One kilometre last century; over two hundred metres in the last five years. For archeologists the disaster had its advantages. Ancient ice was giving up its dead. Hunters, metal prospectors, milkmaids, escaped convicts – the past disgorged in the meltwaters of the present.

"Her body is damaged, you said."

Yvan frowned. "The movement of the ice is destructive. But we are lucky it never fell…"

"She," said Elaine. "She fell."

"Into the accumulation zone. Lower, in the ablation zone, she would have been dismembered."

From the village it was necessary to walk to the crevassed foot of the glacier. She had not expected its surface to look so dirty. Morainic debris, Yvan said. The dark matter was a problem: it reduced the glacier's albedo and hastened its retreat. Elaine heard him talk about negative mass balance and equilibrium but could not concentrate for the physical effort of the climb. Would she dare to search the rucksack for the notebook? What if the flow of ice had destroyed it, or separated it from its owner?

"La morte," said Yvan. "She was a great poet?"

"Good. A very good poet. And unique." She remembered the photograph taken at Garsington: a society beauty, friend of the Lawrences and Robert Graves, who called her Artemis of Bedford Square, the Mistress of Animals. For she had a wildness that called her to the lonely places of Europe, where she hiked and composed strange poems. "It must be possible," Alice had written in that last letter home, "to find a new language, one not of conquest but of surrender to the world. I want to pitch my tent in the mouth of the wild, to hear in my sleep and in my waking the language of nature."

Elaine tried to steel herself for the encounter. To come so close to a revenant! Had Alice heard that wild language? Had she managed to consign it to paper?

"It will make," Yvan said, "the perfect ending for your book."

Elaine felt her cheeks burn. There was a knowingness in his grin that displeased her, and she said nothing until they reached the terminus. There, she was surprised to find a gendarme sunning himself. Behind him stood a tent of reflective material. All about the meltwater there were shreds of cloth and scattered bone.

"Vous êtes prête?"

"Just a minute." Elaine was having difficulty catching her breath. "Can I have a moment with her?"

Later, in the bar of the auberge, Yvan would describe the encounter to his colleagues. He would praise the anglaise for her sangfroid: how she gazed in silence at the distorted face, at the teeth exposed like a snarl and the eroded nose. He would tell how he and the gendarme retreated a little way and watched her kneel beside the body. How she could not get her fingers inside the frozen clothes. How she searched inside the rucksack and found a carnet. And then began to cry. Like that, in front of perfect strangers.

"What was in this notebook?"

"Nothing."

"No writing?"

"No pages. Only the leather binding. I didn't say anything, but the poet had spent two weeks on her own in the mountains. She would have had better uses for paper than writing verses."

With that, Yvan made the gesture of wiping himself between the legs, lady fashion.

At the top of the auberge, in the shuttered darkness of her room, Elaine heard the laughter of the mountaineers.

At prayer in the madhouse with Kit Smart

"I'd as lief pray with Kit Smart as anyone else."
Dr Samuel Johnson

You do me a kindness, sir, to visit me in my dejection. I must receive you in this parlour – it is a fine place is it not? (Do not let it deceive you: within, our condition is not so happy.) Thank you, I believe they are in health. My two boys continue in Latin – I borrowed money of my keeper to pay for it. (Is he gone? Are you quite certain? Then forgive me, I am more comfortable on the floor.) I understand from *Gentleman's Magazine* that my poems live on without me and, indeed, that Mr Arne has set my pastoral hymn to music, alas I shall not profit from it, it is as though I were dead already and no more to be acknowledged for my labours than the cow that furnishes the dinner table. Pray do not, if it please you, rub your foot against the carpet, it upsets the grain and must be rubbed back into contentment. Now tell, does the tongue of slander still wag against me? Slander, sir! I do not use the word loosely. My enemies accuse me of false piety; call me one of Mother Needham's favoured clients. You know I abhorred a bawdy house – except on occasion, when drink had the better of me. But that was in the past, before my illness and second birth. The Lord saved me that I might sing His praises. Oh, I wasted time making enemies with my pen! I was like your namesake the playwright who would rather lose his friend than lose a jest. They did the same to poor Will Preston: he railed against the magistrates' courts and the King's Bench had him confined. A *very* convenient disturbance of wits. But forgive me: isolation makes me harp too much on myself. How goes Mrs Thrale? A most excellent woman – I know you love her – as she does you. In all propriety! Nay, do not leave so soon! My tongue runs away from me, it has so little occasion of exercise. Pray forgive me. Sit a while. You have not brought a little, ah, rum? No matter, no matter. I am so parched I dream of fountains. Ah, we shall drink some day in the light of the sun – just as soon as I am forgiven, though what sin I have committed I know not, they say I am mad, it is not so, for I am composing. They shall be like the songs of David! They will bless and be inquisitive of the Lord! All things that breathe praise God, Mr Johnson. Did He not create the world by speaking it? So a lion that roars himself from head to tail speaks God's word for lion. And a snail is God's word in the shape of his shell – do you see? It is God's work that speaks of God. How else can we speak Him save through His creatures? For I have translated the Psalm:

> The earth is God's, with all she bears
> On fertile dale or woody hill;
> The compass of the world declares
> His all efficient skill.

What think you of it? I shall so punch my words that the mind will take up the image from the mould which I have made. Slow down, yes. I must slow down. Do not think these ravings, sir. I have been deprived of the world that I may comprehend it better. For I bless God that I am not in a dungeon and may see the light of day. Yet even here, the fiend has his agents that will keep me from praising. They lock me in the dark till I am silent. But what may a man do in darkness save people it with his voice? Or else they strap me in my cell to keep me from falling to my knees, but that is not so cruel, for I commune with my own heart and am still. Does this strike you as madness? Though I have a greater compass of mirth and melancholy than another – is that a reason to strap a man to his bed, to chain him in darkness and force harp, harp, harping-irons in his mouth? I would be as a dog, of no consequence. Then perhaps they will not torment me. Men will feed a dog, will they not; they will pat it on the head? No dog is treated as I am. Ah, I shall not weep. I shall not. I am sorry that I roused you from your sleep that time. But I felt the glory of God – we prayed and blessed the Lord, did we not, Mr Johnson, till day broke? I beg you, bring me paper. No, it is not forbidden. But they will not furnish me at my request. Bring me paper. For jubilation to travel it must have transport. How else can my blessings escape these walls? Do me this kindness, sir. And we shall pray, as my cat prays when he licks his paws. Lord, be merciful unto Your creatures. Bless my subscribers. As Your son cured the lunatic, be merciful to all my brethren and sisters in these houses. Bless above all this Your servant, who has agreed to furnish me with the means of spreading my song that will be to Your glory and the praise of all Creation. So be it, Lord. Hallelujah and amen.

Endnotes

1. The Grainger family history was commissioned by Sir Peter Grainger in 1988. Its author remains unknown.
2. Both enquiries into the fire at the ancestral family home proved inconclusive.
3. Virgil Grainger, *A Childhood in Hell*, Harper Collins, London, 2009. The incest chapter was omitted in subsequent editions.
4. Almost certainly fictitious.
5. The damage to the brick wall can still be seen in the front court of Magdalene College, Cambridge. Professor Boyd declined to press charges.
6. Letter to The Times, 26th January 1997.
7. The Guy Burgess Club was set up in Cambridge by Grainger and his friend Andrew Latham-Turner. It continues to this day, its initiation rituals clouded in secrecy. There is no way of proving that our current Prime Minister, Chancellor of the Exchequer, Foreign Secretary, Chief of Staff of the Armed Forces, Archbishop of Canterbury, Head of MI5, Chairman of the CBI and the Board of Governors of the BBC are former members.
8. Grainger never denied that publicity from his million pound advance helped generate sales.
9. Timberlake Hunter, writing in the books section of the Independent on Sunday. Grainger responded furiously to the allegations of plagiarism and Hunter retracted them shortly before entering a Trappist monastery.
10. Grainger's cousin resigned as chairman of the panel of judges.
11. Cassandra Jones was Grainger's fifth literary agent in as many years. She committed suicide in the summer of 2006.
12. Sir Peter could not keep quiet, declaring to the Telegraph, "I don't know who got the little bastard but I can't believe I had anything to do with it."

13. Grainger's investment in various private armies is well documented in Andrew Latham-Turner's *Soldiers of Fortune*, Flamand Press, New York, 2019.
14. Grainger's pamphlet, *Why War is Necessary: a Commonsense View* (The Heritage Foundation, Washington D.C.) was reprinted nine times between 2003 and 2007.
15. Regularly for the National Review and the Spectator.
16. For instance: "I never claimed to be a neo-conservative. I knew they were wrong from the outset and made great efforts to set them right. But what can you do with a bunch of former Trotskyites except nod and smile and try to contain them?" (Prospect, January 2009)
17. Badiou has since renewed her allegations that she was the ghostwriter of Grainger's "comeback" trilogy.
18. The elephant's head was stuffed in Nairobi and shipped back to Nether Compton. See *The Last Great Game Hunter*, Nicholas Gaston, Plum Tree, London, 2029.
19. It is certainly true that a large donation was made at this time to the orphanage in Phnom Penh.
20. His daughter has never spoken publicly on the subject.
21. The most detailed work is by the Romanian journalist Nikolai Comanescu, who spent seven years on Grainger's trail and interviewed many of his lovers, colleagues and victims across three continents. See *The Human Whirlwind: Virgil Grainger by those who knew him*, translated by Nina Hawkes, Oxford, 2027.
22. Grainger admitted, in a late interview with the author, that he had written speeches for his "friends" at Exxon Mobil and Halliburton.
23. Letter to the author from Grainger's oncologist, Dr Janus Gray.
24. Grainger's conversion surprised friends and family alike. Father Dmitri was later convicted of war crimes committed during the Bosnian conflict.
25. Controversy still abounds regarding his final resting place. Nikki, his seventh wife, insists that the ashes were scattered at the

roots of a date palm in the centre of his island in Dubai, but the Grainger family claims that he was buried under a walnut tree at Nether Compton. In the words of his biographer, Nathan Wilson-Grainger: "He may have been a bastard but he was *their* bastard. The family wanted him where they could keep an eye on him…"